Apples & Oranges

Apples & Oranges

Slava Korin

Slava Korin

CONTENTS

CONTENTS

To both sets of grandparents who made it to "till death do us part."

Preface

According to the National Radio Astronomy Observatory in Socorro, New Mexico: on September 2, 2021, astronomers pieced together the fascinating history of a centuries-long death dance between two massive stars which existed 500 million-light-years away. Most stars much more massive than our sun, are born as a binary pair. They closely orbit each other around their common centre of gravity. One of these was more massive than the other and evolved through its normal, nuclear fusion-powered lifetime more quickly. At one point in their history, about three hundred years ago, the smaller of the two moved into the orbit of the larger; an interaction began, which released gas into space. The ejected gas, spiraling outward, formed an expanding, donut-shaped ring, called a torus, around both stars. In the hopes of stellar merger, one neutron star made its way inward to the second star's core. It disrupted the nuclear fusion that was enabling the second star to shine, and that was keeping its core from collapsing under its own gravity. Without fusion, the second star's core did collapse and exploded as a supernova, engulfing them both and expelling several solar masses of material, releasing gravitational potential energy and lighting up outer space. Also, unleashing a barrage of cosmic rays which reached us and those astronomers looking on.

They collided with a silent boom, the glow of a fluorescent light, buzzing timorously above their heads. The smell of fresh hot sweet-sauced pizza, extra cheese, wafting out of the glass display surrounding them like a tantric perfume. The whole world shook, it seemed, when her shoulder fell into his chest and gasped when their bodies were no longer touching.

"Sorry-was that my fault!" Nate gave first only to be ignored as Kate straightened her posture and moved to a further position in front of the pizza counter. It was more of a mishap than a collision. A bump in the night, 3AM and they had just exited the nightclub across the street moving through the air outside, almost as warm as the hot inside the club, except the breeze from the ocean kept slicing it with a cool authority, and into the pizza shop just across the street. They weren't in the club together; in the club at the same time, never actually running into one another in amongst the reveling crowds until, in her drunkenness, she stepped back and bumped into Nate, who was desperately waiting to order. He noticed her bleached platinum hair first, the shine of the overhead fixture showing in white, revealing her chestnut brown roots, the white-tipped bangs dipping down to her brow and curling wisps layered all around her face in a wolf cut, very trendy, popular in the Korean pop scene at the time and a bold choice for a Miami girl, but Kate was always bold. A tiny gold cross hung modestly around her neck, shined with just a glint. He stared at her, admiring her lithe form in the carnal pink crepe-de-chine dress she wore, hanging on thin delicate straps from her shoulders, ending below her knees, tanned calves showing and finishing in delicate silver double-strap shoes. She was probably, actually, the most beautiful girl he had ever seen, radiant and perfect, emanating like the source of all beauty- a headwater for all the good in the world. He was tripping on ecstasy, hard. Everyone looked better at that moment — she had light.

"Did I say sorry?" She had noticed him earlier, before the mash and chose not to turn to face him until that moment.

"You didn't."

"Are you hurt?"

"Hurting. You're really beautiful."

"I think your high. Right. Let's see those pupils." She grabbed his face and his knees buckled slightly. He focused into her icy blue eyes, intent upon making her fall in love as she focused into his swells almost completely blacked-out, just a narrow rim of golden-brown vibrating against the white of his eyeballs.

"You're really high. Your pupils are completely dilated... you look like a big kitten."

"Meow."

"Cute."

"Can I kiss you?"

"Really, really high. But I'm not that drunk, and you should know better than to kiss a stranger. "

"You're actually falling for me."

"I fell on you, not for you."

"No kiss then?"

"Let's exchange numbers and see where it leads us."

"305..."

"First– what's your name?"

"Nate."

"Nice to meet you, Nathan. I'm Kate."

"Kate. And Nate."

"Not yet."

Nate already had his phone in his hand and flipped it open when Kate swung her baguette bag off her shoulder to find her phone. To their surprise, they both had the Startac from Motorola, a little black flip-up that looked like a spy phone, a reckoning of technology meant to keep everyone connected at all times if possible.

"We have the same phone."

"Must be a sign."

"We're soulmates."

"Ecstasy, right? What kind?"

"Buddha's smile."

"Haven't tried those."

"You party?"

"I'm a phony... I just like feeling good."

"It's all alive."

"I know, but it's too much for me sometimes."
They exchanged numbers. The chatter of other patrons rose around them and the guy behind the counter finally turned to Kate to ask for her order.

"What are you having miss?"

"One plain cheese. Fuck it—with pepperoni. And a Coke."

"Pepperoni?"

"Don't stress me already."

"Can I get a bottled water?" Nate focused on the pizza guy and squeezed in his order, then added, "I'll get this."

"I bumped into you," Kate said with a feigned surprise.

"Most action I've had all week and anyway I'm expecting to be in love with you for a long time."

"Jessie- Do you want a slice?" Kate directed her attention to a figure shadowed at her right side. "This is my friend Jessie." She turned to Nate. "Jess this is Nate."

Nate and Jess were not instantly amused, smiling languidly at each other.

"I have some friends as well—I'd rather you didn't meet them just yet."

"Are they trouble?"

"They're just really stupid right now."

"Just a Diet Coke," Jess interjected loud enough for the pizza guy to hear. The pizza was sliced and served in only moments, followed by the drinks, placed with a clink, clink and thud on top of the glass case.

"So, I'm going to call you, definitely. You understand that right?"

"I understand. Not too soon though. Play it cool for a while."

"I'll try." Nate patted Kate on the shoulder, with an adoring farewell sentiment and walked out of the pizza shop to meet a grouping of three other guys standing just outside. Geometric Art Deco buildings sat side by side across the street, their neon signs whispering. The blue-violet sky was lit by a full moon, glimmering stars above and the ocean roared just two blocks east, as they moved away from the pizza shop, cheering and hooting at Nate who beamed brightly with a smile and victoriously shook the hand holding his cellphone in the air.

2

Kate

As soon as Nate walked out of the pizza shop, Kate looked down at her phone, gave it a squeeze and dropped it into her baguette purse. Jessie was guzzling her Diet Coke with a wild thirst for what seemed like minutes before Kate finally reached for her pizza and soda.

"Let's move to a counter- I'm starving."

"It looks so good."

"Split it with me?"

"I can't have pizza!"

"But I can?"

"You're on a supermodel diet. That guy is really a

cutie. Do you know him?"

"Just met."

With that Kate bit firmly into the pointed corner of the slice and let her eyes roll down shut with the hot flavor. It only took a few minutes to finish the slice even with some cheese-picking and chatting. Overall, the night seemed a success and by 3:30AM Jessie and Kate were in a car service headed back to Coral Gables, the town where both grew up together as bestest friends. Kate was dropped off first in front of a white Spanish colonial style casa with arched doorways and blooming red azaleas crouched under the triptych windows on each side of the entrance. At the heavy wooden door, Kate turned back to Jessie and waved with a smile. Inside, she quickly took off her shoes and tiptoed up the stairs and into her room. She still lived with her parents.

The need to shower was evident in the sticky glistening of her skin and after a sniff of her own underarm, she pulled her clothes off and walked into her adjoining bathroom, turned the shower head on, selecting a position for the handle slightly past the middle, closer to the red notch on the shower valve. She reached under the spray to feel the temperature, warm. Good enough, she thought, pulled her panties off (the only article of clothing she was still wearing), and stepped into the tub under the raining shower head. A few good slightly aggressive pumps of the grapefruit body wash, she rubbed her hands together, transforming the gel into a lather, and smoothed it onto her right arm, over the shoulder, then left, rubbing into her armpits after each stroke. Softly over the breasts and flat tummy, she let the suds pour down her legs. Forcing a groan with the puissance she had left, she lifted her right leg up, bending tightly at the knee and lathered it with sweeping motions of her hand, then left she lathered more quickly. With her right hand, she reached her groin and gently washed herself from the front, then her behind, turning to let the stream onto her back and buttocks. The water felt good, and she stood for a while under the stream, mostly thinking about Nate. *He might be the one-silly, she thought—a pizza shop?* At that time, Kate was a psychology student at University of Miami, fourth year, soon to graduate, then she leaves the nest. She had an uncle, her father's brother, who was severely alcoholic and depressed. No one was sure if he was depressed because he was an alcoholic or an alcoholic because he was depressed, but during the holidays when everyone was drinking, he seemed normal and happy. He died young, when Kate was just a little girl. Nobody talked about his condition or much about him after his death. She kept a photo of him at a family Christmas party sipping a Manhattan with a maraschino cherry, a cocktail her mother made for him instead of the whiskey straight he had asked for. In the photo Kate is giving her uncle a kiss under the mistletoe, hoping she would get the cherry still swimming in his tumbler. The sweet smell of the liquor mixed with vermouth and somehow the red maraschino (which she was gifted) with its chloride, sulfur and high fructose syrup has lasted in her memory. Uncle Eddie was the happiest person that Christmas and the Manhattan became his favorite cocktail. He passed shortly after leaving Kate with a certain amount of restive pining which kept her most often single. Kate hadn't dated anyone seriously since high school and didn't want to; her career came first. She didn't want to say that she wouldn't date anyone until she graduated college, at least, although it worked out that way. No one really since she started university with the exception of a guy she had met sophomore year. A very nice guy who reminded her of her uncle, and after watching him drink through their first two dates, leaving just a sloshy blur of their conversation, she decided celibate wasn't a bad idea; she mixed her new self-awareness with egotism and a desire to achieve contentment, and decided to wait for a suitable boyfriend. If you consider celibate healthy, then she had a healthy mind frame, however, that didn't stop her from going out occasionally with Jessie who would guard her from unwanted affections until this night out. She thought to wash her hair quickly, rinsing out the smell of the club and pizza shop, forgetting the conditioner. With her eyes closed, she reached for a fluffy towel and wrapped herself in it, tucking the corner of her towel at her chest, with it covering her legs to mid thigh. With another towel she dried her hair with fervor, hung it on a towel rod and walked back into the bedroom, feeling the coolness of the chilled air-conditioned air on her skin.

When she finally made it to her bed wearing just a pair of cotton undies and her favorite already faded and soft tshirt from Madonna's *The Drowned World Tour*, she grabbed her purse, pulled out the phone and quickly punched in the letters N-A-T and Nate's phone number appeared on her phone screen in black digital on a greenish-grey face. She held the phone in front of herself and stared at it intently hoping it would decide for her, but there was really nothing to decide. "He's the one," she whispered and pressed send. One buzzing ring, then another and finally an electronic voice, an intercept message stating that, "this number is no longer in service." Her eyes welled up with tears thick enough to cloud her vision and she hung-up and pressed send again only to receive the same message. She must have entered his number incorrectly or he was just messing with her head. He wasn't just playing around with her, she insisted, placed the phone on her nightstand and laid back against her pillows. The room wasn't too cold, it was still and quiet, and she fell asleep on top of her covers listening to the thin distant ringing in her ears, residue from the music in the club, before she could cry.

3

Nate

Nate was the last one left on the beach. He insisted on staying after his friends left for their respective apartments across Miami Beach. The carousing had reached a high point when Johnny Diaz ran into the ocean naked at around 5AM. After Johnny dried off with his shirt, he also departed, shouting back at Nate from Ocean Drive with a hopeful invitation, "Breakfast at the diner?" Which was refused. Nate was the only one who decided to wait for the sun. He lived on the other side of the beach in a modern tower facing Biscayne Bay; in one of the apartments his father had accumulated through his mediocre real estate ventures, providing a comfortable life for his son, Nate, who also dallied in real estate, after finishing an art program up north in New York with little difficulty and avoiding the interior design program his father insisted upon and instead settled for a regular Bachelor of Fine Arts, that lost its luster after a few months of job hunting, sending Nate back to Miami less hopeful than before. Nate's father had wanted to make use of Nate's artistic ability, in order to flip properties, and when he returned to Miami, he settled on real estate associate in his father's realty, and they did manage to flip a few properties with the help of a professional interior designer, and some of his own artistic savvy. The same interior designer decorated his apartment, where he had witnessed many sunsets from his fifteenth-floor scenic window, but he had never really seen a sunrise on the beach, until this morning. The same decorator, a gaunt and elegant Russian woman with dark hair, was Nate's last serious girlfriend. One of the many episodes from his serial monogamy. It didn't work out between them simply because she wanted marriage. He wanted a diverting relationship, some laughs and good sex, someone to hold, hopefully warm with lovingkindness and affection. The sex with Jenia was good, but the Miami sun always outdid her in warmth, leaving her as pallid as her unnaturally white skin would suggest. After a few design assignments and many dates, she anticipated a proposal that he would not make, instead offering a handshake, rather than asking for her hand. Jenia had style and significant allure, but her heart seemed to be in the wrong place, beating to the rhythm of scheduled success, which Nate already felt in his father's accomplishments. Not any less valid than true love, at least not in the contemporary schematic which has introduced pic and swipe, or the old-world order of arranged marriages; difficult to digest for a romantic idealist like Nate who grew up watching Hughes teenage movie romances from the eighties on DVD; movies he was urged to watch by his older cousin, a modern day hippie who ended up marrying a French girl while studying in Paris, and claimed that the soul of America was dying—that we had begun to loose faith in love, slowly, sex and lasciviousness was overwhelming our innocence and gentility. *The Breakfast Club* was his favorite; not that he was ever really a delinquent, however he did to expect to find love awkwardly as some of his sexuality was unresolved.

It was the first glimpse of golden light which reminded Nate of his new-found love interest, beautiful Kate. The golden yellow rising into an amusing orange bordered a more expansive section of sky in a slate blue. A blue that reminds one of the stormy blue of clouds before a rain and then further up into the midnight color. He remained seated in the sand just a hundred feet from the thin rolling waves, each attempting to reach him with some vigor only to be disappointed by the distance between him and the wetted sand. When the midnight evaporated from the sky and the blues really began to burn, the bright hot ball at the horizon making an entrance, he felt a warm urgency rise within him, a novel feeling which made the skin on his unclad arm unexpectedly rise in goosebumps and the light behind his eyes glow with intention. When the whole of the star shown in the sky, just a few minutes after it was first set ablaze, Nate decided to avoid the cooler sensibility of modern courtship and pulled his phone from his pant's pocket. It was after the third ring that he finally felt relief, upon hearing Kate's sleepy voice answer with a grumbling sweet, "Hello." "Good morning," Nate said cheerfully with a long night's rasp curling his words.

"I couldn't imagine waiting the appropriate amount of time to call you."

"I didn't really want you to wait any respectable amount of time. Where are you?"

"I'm watching the sunrise on the beach."

"That's beautiful."

"Can I see you later today?"

"Sure. I just need to get some sleep first."

"I'll call you later."

4

Nate arrived at the restaurant early in eager anticipation and found Kate already standing at the host podium, her back was turned to him, but it was her, in cream paints and a chocolate camisole, mostly hidden by her hair, leaving her golden shoulders visible.

Let me see your face. Let me hear your voice, for your voice is sweet, and your face is lovely.

Her scent, lavender mixed with the ocean breeze, touched him first.

"Kate?" he said aloud, and she turned from the dark-skinned Cuban hostess to face him without surprise.

The voice of my beloved! Behold, he comes, leaping on the mountains, skipping on the hills.

"You're here. We're both early."

"I've been waiting all my life."

"Stop being so dramatic, it's just a first date."

"First date then. Let's see how it goes."

"Exactly. We're both here." She turned her head to the hostess.

"Party of two."

Let him kiss me with the kisses of his mouth; for your love is better then wine.

Dinner on the Tuesday following their Saturday night stumble, was at a delightful seafood restaurant near the water, several blocks north of Nate's sunrise. For their first date they decided to meet at Aquagrille, a mostly white interior with lowlight and the sound of lounge music melting into the waves past the sand. Kate drove across the crossway onto the beach and Nate arrived in a car service from the other side of the island. She promised herself she wouldn't drink, and he expected to be engaged by spring.

When they took their seats at a table against the wall, she sat on the cushy banquette and he in the chair across from her. She smiled as soon as they were facing one another; a cool warmth like a kiss on a chilly day, wiped away by a casual breeze. It reminded him of French salons and what Marie Antoinette's giggle would have sounded like. Nate looked at her wanting more than her gaze, catching her glance and into her eyes.

Your eyes are doves behind your veil.

Then his eyes looked on her mouth, a sweet ruby red pout broaching her golden veneer.

Your lips are like scarlet thread. Your mouth is lovely.

"Will you marry me?"
"Not yet. What's your favorite color?"
"Green."
"Serenity. Nice."

"What's yours?"

"Blush."

"Pretty."

There was a silence between them which was ruined by the waiter's cheerful introduction. They ordered drinks and asked for more time with the menu. Nate watched Kate scan the menu and smiled at her glimmer of hope, herb-crusted fish. She ordered it with delight when the waiter returned with their drinks. A gin highball for Nate and a freshly opened bottle of sparkling water for Kate, she immediately said, "We can share the sparkling. I'm not going to drink all this water, or I'll be tinkling all night."

"Tinkling?"

"I'm bloated already," she added.

"You look beautiful."

"That's sweet, you look nice as well. Better sober. Your eyes were so big the other night. Now you look presentable."

"Presentable to who?"

"I'm just saying that sobriety suits you."

He returned by taking a gulp of his gin and smiling.

"Not for long."

"Let's keep it tame tonight."

They decided to talk throughout dinner, and it was Kate who began bluntly with a modernly sober question.

"Are we ready to survey each other's sex partner history? Isn't that the thing now?"

"Past partners and test results? I think that was the 90's."

"No, I think that is still now. What else could it be?"

"It could be that we just see where this goes."

"I thought you were in love?"

"Desperately."

"Ok, then. I've been single the past couple years."

"I'm clean as well. I came out of a relationship a few months ago — still friends, and I had a routine checkup just last month."

"So, nothing since last month?"

"Earlier, but I had the checkup last month."

"That's good. We're safe."

"If we stay monogamous."

"Look who's jumping the gun?"

"I wanted to beat you to the punch."

"Now then, what do you do you?"

Nate explained that he was a real estate person. She said that she imagined him in some sort of romantic profession. He confessed his artistic leanings and informed her of his BFA with some pride. She connected, stating that Jessie's older brother, (you remember Jess), works at an advertising agency in New York.

"I wish I would have known you back then. It would have saved me some of the pain of rejection," he said.

"He started at the agency just recently."

"Well then, that wouldn't have worked."

"How long ago did you stop chasing your dream?"

"I found a new one." She knew that he meant her.

Then they discussed Kate's studies in psychology. She picked at her flaky fish and after her third forkful, a passing nervous thought, she stated, "Fish is an excellent brain food."

"The abundance of omega3," he said.

"...it sharpens the memory and keeps the brain from decline."

"I'll try to eat more fish," Nate responded splitting a lobster ravioli with his fork.

"That looks delicious."

"It is. Would you like one?"

"Just one." Kate edged her plate closer to his plate for transfer of one lobster ravioli. A quick bite and she made a yummy humming noise with the top of her mouth.

"So good." Then she entreated Nate with, "I'm planning on moving up to New York for graduate school."

"Oh, really? How long do we have?"

"It depends."

"What school?"

"New York University."

"I used to walk through Washington Square Park almost every day."

"Would you want to move back there?"

"I think my father would be upset, but maybe some day I'll give it another try."

"I think he'd be happy for you."

Just before dessert arrived, a delicious lava cake

that they also shared, they decided to seriously consider the move up north without blatantly confessing to a future together.

"I can't resist. I'm getting the first bite," Kate said reaching the middle of their table to slice off a piece of the cake. It was all gone in a few minutes, just the fudge on their forks and a smear on the plate left as evidence. The bill came promptly after Nate finished his last sip of warm gin and although Kate glanced at it, she chose not to put up a fight. "Next time, dinner is on me," she said. She did offer him a ride back to his home, without any presumption.

When they pulled up to Nate's tower he asked unashamedly if Kate would like to see his apartment. She responded that it was too soon and that she trusted that he lived well enough for them to continue their courting. They kissed briefly and enthusiastically, trying to preserve as much as possible for the next time they kissed. She waited for the moment to finish with the last satisfying sensation before their lips were apart again; before running her pink-nailed fingers in his dark short-cropped hair, up over the top of his head and trickling them down the front of his face. "Now we're together."

5

The second date was completely without pretension as they had already decided that they were going to fall in love, dismissing any other choice in the matter. Love it would be. A night out at the movies, holding hands in the dark watching a modern romance. Like that! They exclaimed silently. We want to love completely in an addiction so powerful that not even amnesia could erase us from one another. Giddy, swaying, overwhelming entanglement. Agreed, and they squeezed their palms together tighter, disregarding the warm moistness, formed by the hour or so of handholding in the theater. That night Kate did join Nate in his apartment, and they had their first intercourse. Kate pulled Nate's tshirt up and off his lean body moments after they entered the apartment. He stood still a few feet from the sofa, while she kissed his chest dulcetly, and when she reached for a kiss from his lips, he wrapped his arms around her. They blindly found the bedroom and fell onto the bed, only allowing themselves to breathe heavily during the first embraces. The low moans began after they found a physical familiarity and an echoing simultaneous guffaw upon orgasm.

She stayed the night and was awoken by Nate's pecking lips.

"Do you want some breakfast?"

"I want to sleep."

"It's 9am already. Time to get out of bed."

"It's Sunday."

"I have breakfast ready – waffles."

"You made waffles?"

"With berries."

"I'll get up then."

The open kitchen facing expansive windows looked out onto Biscayne Bay with boats speckling their green blue water that morning, already. Nate finished pouring coffee into the two mugs he had chosen; his regular Koons mug with the inflatable Hulk image, and for Kate he selected a white stoneware mug with glazed bottom. After filling them and the creamer, he carried them over to the dining table, just as Kate slid into a seat. The waffles sat in the middle of the table still steaming towards the ceiling.

"There you are."

"This looks incredible."

"It's just waffles."

"I've never had homemade waffles."

"Always a first."

"So, that was good right?"

"Last night? Last night was excellent."

"That's settled."

"Were you worried?"

"It would not have mattered too much, but what a blessing."

"Blessing? You're exaggerating."

"I couldn't stand it if we ended up just friends."

"We're much more than friends."

With that she picked up a fork and helped herself to a waffle, added berries and poured some syrup, before he could offer to serve her. She already had a mouthful by the the time Nate tasted his first sip of coffee.

"So good." She hummed out the side of her full mouth.

"Eat up." He waited another two sips, looked out the windows at the sun glistening on the water, then served himself a waffle with enthusiasm.

6

By the end of the month Kate had ownership of Nate's top dresser drawer and the contents changed from undies and tube socks to panties and bras, mixed in with her favorite lounge pants and a few tees. Her toothbrush had its own slot and somehow her face wash found a position inside his medicine cabinet, right next to his moisturizer. She was sleeping over at Nate's more than at her own home, and after the slightest persuasion, she was gifted a set of keys on their two-month anniversary and finally moved in two weeks later when they couldn't find a reason as to why she shouldn't.

Once they were settled in together, (Kate with a whole dresser and closet to herself) after some paring down and inaudible griping by Nate, they found a balance in a shared living space, matching his work schedule to Kate's school and study habits in an attempt to couple as well as possible. The cleaning lady visited twice a week and left no chores other than filling the dishwasher. All their time together was meant for them to be together, to prompt actual scintillating neurological love which they already experienced, however the habit of which, the day-to-day coddling and coaxing, sentiment and security of actualized love was still baking like a soufflé. The tiptoeing was evident in tiny kisses and unnerved glances stemming from something as trivial as a grumpy grumbling morning. Love is after all at a much higher consideration, it would have to be, to lift us up on its angel wings and harpsichord strings. Devoid of the reality of our clumsy physicality, lying right up on top with the superlative, allowing for even the nastiest, beastliest of us to touch it when we are willing to give something of ourselves, envelop someone else in our personal shield of pride and vanity in an empathic bond, not necessarily sexual, although it is the physical that allows us to taste it and fly higher. However, there sometimes lies distrust - we begin to consider our other and love itself doubtfully, simply because love has no human body, no visible form other than in our thoughts, actions and re-actions, still and luckily tied to the material world. We are held down by inaccuracy and misconceptions, imperfections that keep our dance from flight and our song from light. They were making a go of it, attempting the most beautiful accord, sincerely hoping that fate wasn't just toying with them. The next step was to have the big talk, about skeletons in the closet and lurking demons, just in case something was to arise in the future. There was some natural hesitation for fear of razing what was so delicately built in the past few months, but the decision at the end of an especially comfortable day together was to rummage. Kate couldn't allow one more moment to pass without investigating the closets they hadn't sorted between themselves. When she caught Nate particularly relaxed one weekend afternoon, lying on the sofa with a copy of *Science Today* held firmly, near-sightedly, barely more than a foot away from his face, as he intently read the latest science information there was to offer to the general public— she made her move. She swept by him a couple times, once with a glass of juice, the second just to see if he noticed, which he did with a coy smirk, until she finally decided to attack, which she did with delicious pleasure.

"Now that we're practically hitched...Are there any dark secrets that you're hiding?"

"Not really? Why? Second thoughts?"

"Second thoughts about what?" She pulled the magazine away from his face and rested it on his lap.

"I kissed a boy—a man really, my roommate in college."

"That's not too bad."

"And we masturbated each other after getting stoned, while watching porn on the internet."

"That's a little more intense, but I can handle it."

"But, I'm not gay."

"I didn't say that you were —are."

"I'm not, so don't worry and please don't judge me—I know you're trying to analyze this...it was just stupid."

"I'm not worried. I made out with Jess a few times when we're kids, in high school, and I think we might have tongued each other one night out on the dance floor."

"Thank goodness."

"You thought I was a square?"

"I thought I was some sort of degenerate."

"We're perfectly normal. It's just residual energy from the sexual revolution. Sometimes our bestial Id gets the best of us."

"More than residual...An awakening of some kind —peace, love... a congress of humanity!"

"Are you still awakened?"

"No, just saying that I think it affected... me at least and you–the love generation created a new understanding."

"Do you want us to have an understanding?"

"No, not at all. We're beautiful together."

"That's a relief, because I'm really getting into this."

"We are getting along nicely. I thought you a touch shy at first, but now you're warming up to me."

"Oh, now I'm warming up? Watch out—it might get too hot."

"I'm burning already."

"Good then."

"What else?"

"I told you my uncle was an alcoholic."

"No, you didn't."

"I must have, anyway, that's as dark as it gets and that he died young, and alone. They said from heart failure. I think it was really a broken heart. That's why I decided on psychology. I told you this."

"You didn't, but now I understand."

"So, you'll move up to New York with me and help me devote my life to a greater understanding of the physical effects of our psychology."

It was something she thought about since high school. She wanted to feel the buzz and to plug into the more powerful libidinal energies generated by, and perspicacity of, the big city. Kate was convinced that that was the only way she could completely achieve a successful practice of healing the mind- through its connection to the collective unconsciousness. Tuning, the idea was to tune to the rhythm of the whole, or to connect to, at least, a greater portion of society in order to find the right peg for each person in the balance and counterbalance. A big pool of energy with more variations of psyche and personality would allow a greater understanding of the human mind and each person's quantic value and position in our interrelated existence.

"You want to figure out how his heart was broken."

"Sort of, but more importantly to help other people like him."

"Alcoholics?"

"People with depression. That's really what it is I think, at least from what I've learned so far. It's this dark menacing beast that breaks your will, your heart, and keeps you under its weight until you can't breathe anymore, and you collapse completely."

"That's horrible."

"It is-it can eat up a person's life. Mental illness is the scariest. Losing comprehension...you literally lose your mind."

"I'm not planning on going crazy—just being madly in love."

"Madly in love." Kate tumbled on top of Nate landing her upside-down heart-shaped butt onto his lap, somehow sliding his magazine into the crevice of the sofa.

"With me?"

"With you."

"That's settled then. Now what about moving to New York?"

The conversation about moving didn't have a resolution that Saturday afternoon because as soon as Katie fell into Nate's lap they began kissing. This led them into an afternoon of delight. She still had a few months left before graduation and Nate was working on a flip in Sunny Isles, a small three-bedroom Spanish missionary home in need of restoration. Lots of white paint and some Majorcan tiles in the kitchen which needed to be replicated and replaced. Bathrooms would benefit with modern fixtures, the master with a steam shower. It needed some special attention, more so than the completely contemporary homes his ex remodeled. Speaking of his ex, whom he had cordially encountered maybe twice since finding Kate; they were still friendly—only after Nate gushed about his new girlfriend, did his father decide that he and Jenna needed to be kept apart. This could be the one, Barry Goldman thought, and a psychologist, nonetheless. The homes were split amongst the two of them so that they could focus individually on design and decor. Turned out well, and they were doing twice the work. One of Nate's considerations about moving away from Miami was the job, which he learned to enjoy; after all an applied art like interior design has its own merits as well, combining the high-minded efforts of art with the utilitarian-based needs of design. Leaving would cause a burden on his father, but good thing Jenia was there to help, and she was capable enough. It was love and he had to give it a chance, whether it be in New York or Alaska, if Kate was the one, then he had to follow.

7

Her graduation was lovely. It was held outside on the football field of the university, the lawn freshly trimmed, hundreds of relieved graduating students bright-eyed in their seats, tassels still dangling on the right side of their square-shaped hats. The murmuring sound of the student body hung in the air before the president of the university, a tan fellow in a slate blue suit began to speak out through the microphone with a metallic resonance.

"Welcome students, alumni, family and friends." Murmur became a silent hum, and everyone attenuated to the stage. Nate, who was of course invited, held his seat with a pride he hadn't felt before, next to Kate's parents in the back with his own Sony cyber-shot camera already extended.

They had met before, just before Kate moved in with Nate; dinner at their home in Coral Gables, where Kate grew up. They ate hurriedly without discomfort, rather with the understanding that *"we have a good one here"* and the pork chops took second position. Kate showed him her room and they kissed her first kiss in her childhood bedroom on her cream, pink and mint floral duvet, allowing him to press against her for a few moments as they lay on the bed. Now, they all sat together in the late spring heat, sun blazing from its almost noon position with an eager intensity. Her mother, Dolores, attempted to smile continuously while her father, George, rubbed the lens of his Nikon with serious resolve and in anticipation. "Katherine Randolph," echoed throughout the field. When Kate rose to accept her Bachelor of Science in Psychology, Kate's mother's hands began to clap against each other furiously in a thunderous roar that silenced the rest of the audience. Her father hollered out, "Katie! Katie!" And Nate almost leapt into the air with his camera pressed against his eye, depressing the shutter-release button continuously, as she made her way to the stage to accept her diploma.

Her gait was steady and allowed her gown to move softly with each step; she turned to the crowd only once with a short smile, hoping to offer her invitees the perfect photo opportunity, before reaching her hand out to accept her accreditation. The pass off, a handshake, big smiles and four years gone by. Katie continued across the makeshift platform to the other end of the stage where she switched her tassel from right to left before descending six stairs to reach the grass.

At the end of the ceremony, she met her parents and Nate at the fifty-yard line where they coerced Jess to snap a photo of the four of them together. Then one of Jess and Kate squeezing their satins and holding their mortarboard hats, already in hand. Then Nate and Kate hugging tightly. "We're doing this right!" Kate exclaimed. It was too late to change course anyway. Nate's father had someone scout an apartment in New York City for the two of them already: a cozy one bedroom right near Washington square above the Dojo restaurant, next to the Stern business school building. Nate would never need worry.

His first day at the Primum office, Nate or as his new friend and cubicle buddy called him, Nathan, had to find his bearings in a new job, a position he had thought he would not ever have had given his prior momentum. Now, he was a professional artist working as an assistant graphic designer at an advertising agency in big time New York City. Incredible, it seemed that a mishap landed him back on the same cloud his dreams lay upon. A syrupy thought that lingered in his mind throughout most of the day, revealing itself in the many secretive texts he sent to Kate, almost all responses to her concerned questioning.

"How is it?"
"I'm having a good time, so far."
"Did you make friends yet?"

"Just one, Brandon."

"Is Jessie's brother being nice to you?"

"I only saw him once this morning when I first arrived, but it's early."

Kate's sense of responsibility was overwhelming and urgent throughout the day encouraging him to be the best at organizing his desk, the only assignment he had the first day, other than scanning through previous ads and campaigns to get an idea of the agency's aesthetic sensibility. Lush images: a SUV in a perfectly selected citron color, sitting on a dirt mound surrounded by green foliage, monkeys and a parrot nestled in between the branches and leaves, (Rousseau), caught his attention and immediately added enthusiasm to his day. "Anywhere you want to go!" it read below the Michelane CrossClimate tires. Whereas, an empty generic hospital hallway, with the phrase, "Who will be there to take care of you?" added a looming dread that forced him to send a smiley face heartkiss emoji. Then, an actual perfectly painted coral red mouth, and seductively distant eyes hovering above a sculpted nose, as if the lips were no longer part of the face, only resting there for the photograph and the brand's liquid logo firm in a gradually transitioned lavender background. Thousands of files and just as many images with copy and without, some patched together with stock images and others glossy and tuned to a heightened sense by an art department coordinated to make indelible images, powerful moments captured, you'd think solely for the purpose of selling, but rather as a system of societal communication. *Tell me what you want/This is what I've got* - advertising adds the—*Don't you just love it!...* to the marketing equation, enticing the viewer to shop or at least to consider how great the product or momentary concern, augmenting the prestige and potency of the ad, product and brand. Often, the agency is silent. Brandon was not silent, he had been working at the agency as a graphic designer for over two years now, and he had stories to tell, hotter than anything in *MadMen*. Seems that those who tweak our concept of modernity are a rollicking crowd. Big money, big fun as he learned in Brandon's ineffectively whispered voice and moderated tone of phony respect. Nate embraced his new friendship instantly, enjoying chats in the employee lounge and talking through the chipboard cubicle walls like two school kids at a sleepover, huddled under tented sheets flashing light on the higher-ups. Brandon is gay, as they come. A handsome specimen at that, lean muscle and bright slight eyes which he inherited from his Asian mother, his red hair always trimmed, and skin moistened by the finest men's lotions and serums. At only twenty-four he was already a full-fledged graphic designer at Primum with an ear in on office chatter and immersed in the pond of mainstream New York nightlife, gay nightlife specifically, dipping in and out of clubs and bars on a regular basis. A regular butch queen of New York City. It started with a firm handshake, firmer than Nate homophobically expected.

"So nice to have you with us." Brandon smiled brightly with freshly whitened teeth.

"Thanks. I'm looking forward to working with you as well," Nate returned in his goodest manner.

"This is a fun place… lots of late hours though."

"I'm up for it," Nate consoled himself.

"I'm sure you are. If the day is not too hard on you maybe we could enjoy a drink after work."

"That sounds really nice, but I'm meeting my girlfriend after to celebrate my first day."

"Girlfriend, huh?"

"We live together."

"That's very sweet. Maybe some other time then."

"I'd love to, anytime, just not this evening."

His response was not received negatively, and they continued to form a friendly bond, despite his entanglement. Entanglement seems crude, cosmic engagement, fate brought Kate and Nate together and urged them to NYC.

9

Just as Nate was about to catch a cab outside the club, a younger couple in black and acid green colors standing fifty-feet away exuberantly waving, snatched it from him and Kate who were there first, without any acknowledgment. The other couple found seats in the taxi quickly, wickedly giggling to one another, high on something as well. Their cab swooshed by them in a smear of yellow; the other two revelers nestled close together in the back seat. A tiny ripple opened in the electromagnetic pond, spoiling the almost perfected glass surface of their future with vibrating ripples.

"Can you believe that crap? How the hell could they just steal our cab?" He didn't know if he should lower his taxi engaging arm.

"Here's another one..., "Kate uttered. And she began to wave her hand in the air with purpose.

"Where are all those people, my people, who believe in virtue, sanctity of the body and the divinity of mankind's spirit?"

"Shut the hell up sweetie! No one like that left, not even you. Get in the taxi."

"Me, me—I still believe. I believe in love and kindness and..."

"And nothing. You're just high."

"I'm not just high. I'm seeing clearer." Nate followed Kate into the car missing a bump on the head as he slid into a seat and immediately pressed the window control button to lower the window.

"Why are you opening the window? It's December."

"I need fresh air. Are you cold? You have a puffer on."

"I'm not cold— but I don't want you to get sick. Zip up your jacket."

He did zip-up his jacket with a defiant attitude and Kate turned to look out her window after grasping his hand. It was forty-two blocks south and five avenues east to reach their apartment.

That Friday evening began simply enough with an article Nate was reading about bone conduction headphones, again, *Science Today*. Seems as if our bones can hear, vibrations at least and these vibrations can be translated by the inner ear. This new listening device, Mobiwan is able to transmit voice communication directly into the inner ear through micro-vibrations on the head, skull, and bypasses the need for headphones in the ear. Meant for those who need to hear an audible transmission over noise of some kind. Funny enough, our bones are listening in on us, finding ulterior purposes for the sound around us and possibly creating new motives in our bodies, stimulating us in a way we're completely unaware of, tuning when we're not really listening. When Nate shared this factoid with Kate, who herself was involved in folding some laundry, she said, "Let's shake our bones." Seems as if a staleness had settled on them the past few months, something they needed to shake off. A negative entropy of certain relationships, when the romantic attachment becomes completely co-dependent, to the point that nothing else other than being together is a concern. A disintegration into uniformity and a degradation of the purpose of coupling, which I assume is to become better, individually and for one another. When leaving the nest for something becomes an annoying disturbance to the cohabitating, something is wrong. An exertion or effort, whether entertainment, dining or vacationing must be made to keep from becoming stale...and so, they decided to have a night out at a popular nightclub in midtown, Sound Factory, featuring a mostly hetero crowd that was oddly enough greeted by a transvestite, well on her way to becoming a transexual. A premature excursion, as New Year's Eve was just two weeks away, still a wonderful evening, during which they were able to attain two low-grade ecstasy pills from a pixieish young woman who called herself Fairy, with pretty glittering features and pink pigtails, wearing five-inch-thick rubber-soled sneakers and a rainbow on her cropped tshirt. The ecstasy was good enough to make them feel tingly and lovely. They decided to ignore the possibly depressive repercussions of the drug, disregarding work on Monday; they were resolved to enjoy that night, comingling within the mass of bodies on the dance floor, bumping and gyrating, arms escaping the silhouette, reaching into the air. Kate turned away from the car window where she was focusing on the passing streets and Manhattan lights burning and blurred by her high, looked at Nate, and squeezed his hand, anticipating an especially delicious round of lovemaking.

Nate leaned his head back against the hard, cold, cracked vinyl seat, his ears still listening to the whisper of music from the disco. He couldn't keep himself from recalling a Christmas dance he had attended during high school; a private school in Miami, a beautiful campus just inside Coconut Grove, Carrington of the Sacred Heart, where he was one of the many Jewish boys enjoying a well-rounded education. The dance was not an unusual event at the school—what happened was. It was a rousing party held just two days before Winter break in the gymnasium of the school, decorated by a committee, led by the student government, who had garnished it with glittering stars and metallic balloons, in reference to the evening's theme, "Starry Night." Individual water bottles and single-serve chips were offered, even an exaggerated and menacing punch bowl from which no one drank sat impressively with a nostalgic nod. Everyone showed to the party. It would have been ruinous not to attend, however, a date was not required and other than the several couples there, most kids went solo or in groups. Nate arrived with his best friend Johnny Diaz, just in the middle of "The Music Sounds Better With You" by Stardust, an hour after the nine o'clock start of the event, but genuinely enthused, encouraged by the pot they smoked a few minutes earlier around back of the building. Their heightened mood allowed them to absorb the drenching wave of sound as they walked into the space, pulsating throb and synth agitating their neurotransmitters to percolation. Almost everyone there was already clumped on the basketball court moving to the DJ's configuration of songs, added beats and technique. Nate and Johnny found a few of their classmates and began to dance as well. By the time a remix of "Frozen" by Madonna came on, Nate, Johnny and their gathering had worked up a light sweat, shimmering when hit by the imported laser lights, glistening green like alien skin. Nate found a trance in the short spurts of a strobe light which held him, just bouncing from foot to foot, only Johnny's silhouette was visible, streams of light escaping past his dancing form, each shape he expressed celebrated by a flash of light and a beat of the song, freezing lyrics with syncopated blinks in the dark of the gymnasium. Nate thought that Johnny was beautiful at that moment. Johnny's body exerting its dance in a solitary connection to the music was beautiful. The warmth of their friendship was beautiful, and they shared a meaningful intimacy, something cultivated. A moment later, he watched Johnny approach him, releasing the spray of light which silhouetted him. He got so close, Nate thought Johnny was going to kiss him, but instead he reached Nate's ear and barely touched it to say, "Do you want to get a water?" His ear tensed and Nate agreed. They left the dance floor to find a sparkling moment at the snack table.

"We're here, Babe." Kate squeezed his hand again. He shivered out of his recollection and opened the car door. Kate passed a bill to the cab driver and they exited the taxi.

10

One weekend morning in the following month of May, Nate caught Kate working diligently at their dining room table on what looked like an arts & crafts project. Torn magazine pages, scissors and glue scattered flippantly across the top of the table; Kate, her hair in a ponytail held tight by a scrunchie, sipping her coffee, waiting for inspiration while focusing on a few images she had chosen. Nate pretended to ignore her as he walked out of the bedroom, tugged his boxer shorts up higher onto his waist and proceeded to the kitchen to get his own cup of coffee. Good morning, he offered in her direction before he maneuvered behind the kitchen island, reached for the coffee pot and his Whitney Museum mug, and poured himself a cup. Then after a gulp, he said with a fuller expression,

"Whatcha got there?" He peaked from behind the counter.

"I've been working on this all morning," she answered. He then decided to inspect her project and with some confidence, gained through education and experience, moved over to her side where he perused the open pages of a large canvas bound book.

"A collage? Why is there a snake-eyed child in the collage?"

"That's the only photo of a child I could find in *Fashion* in their June issue...and I want lots of children at the wedding. "

"What wedding?"

"Our wedding. You asked me to marry you."

"First date?"

"That's right... at our first real date. Don't you have any nieces and nephews?"

"Lots of them, but I was thinking small wedding, just parents and a few friends."

"That's quaint. I want a real wedding with children running around screeching and leaving ketchup stains on the tablecloths. Any qualms?"

"Lots of snake-eyed demon children. Right. Gotcha."

"That's the only one I could find. I'll get some more magazines."

"I'll get you an engagement ring."

"That would be lovely. Something simple and pretty please. Emerald cut if you can find one."

"Have you heard of lab-grown diamonds. I think they're new."

"Around since 1954."

They were engaged. Not officially just yet, they would have to wait for the ring, nevertheless, it was palpable now and Kate's bride's book was to become her Bible for the next few months. She clipped everything that reminded her of love or marriage in whites and pinks. A bright-eyed starlet holding wildflowers in a prairie, her pastoral georgette and lace dress aglow, lit by a distant sun. Sweet-looking cream puffs stacked high into a pyramidal amuse-bouche. Flowers, flowers and more flowers of every kind. The goal was blushing bride.

...then comes marriage.

It was decided that the wedding would be held, ceremony and festivities both at Nate's parents' home, Barry and Ruth Goldman's estate in Coconut Grove. A rather large contemporary home, brutalist with curtain wall windows facing out onto the deck and backyard, really a lawn, which reaches into the Atlantic Ocean with a private dock. Not quite Louis Kahn, yet an utterly modern building. Nate called it an institution until he grew old enough to appreciate the minimalism of the modernist movement in architecture, then as a teenager he was allowed a few parties and now he and Kate were to be married in the cooler month of February, not quite on Valentine's Day because it fell on a Thursday that year, but the Sunday after. It had to be in Miami, after all, their family and friends were in Miami, and honestly, New York had not impressed home on them just yet. The winter was too sharp sometimes and they missed the familiarity of a southern sunshine, but there was nothing like a Northeastern pumpkin-hued autumn, with bright crisp blue skies or the tingle of warmth in a dewy spring morning. The cooler climate allowed them to form an intricate crystalline bond, stimulated by downtown restaurants and uptown museums. The Miami sun would warm their hearts.

The day of the wedding finally arrived. The institution became wedding central with different rooms assigned for different purposes. Nate in his old room. Kate in the guest room with her mother and make-up artist. Ruth moved about all day from the lawn to kitchen ensuring that all the instructions were followed by a generous staff of caterers and decorators. Barry and George sat on Barry's boat smoking cigars and listening to seventies dad rock. Kate had chosen pink lillies,

Lily Speciosum, an oriental variety, and they were everywhere; as centerpieces mixed with bouquet filler and adorning the wooden chuppah, wrapped in white silk cloth. It was going to be perfect. She just had just one question she wanted to ask her mother before becoming betrothed. She started by asking the make-up artist to leave for a few minutes, as politely as she could before anything other than the concealer was put on, then, she turned to her mother, who sat peering into the same mirror from the edge of the bed, and simply asked, "Why did Uncle Gabe die alone." It seemed as if she decided not to wait for her own psychologically resolved answer and the pre-ceremony jitters rumbling in her gut gave her an aggravated potency.

"Katie, your uncle was gay. We all knew it. He told me once when he was in high school that he liked a friend of his. A close friend he used to idle with. It didn't work out, they stopped spending time together and he cried and never opened up again. He had a few girlfriends after, but not love, not like what he wanted or how we imagine it to be. He loved you very much though. You were his little angel."

Dolores stood and walked the few steps over to Kate, kissed her daughter on the forehead and rubbed her arm softly.

"I hope you've found love with Nate."

"There's no one else for me, Mom."

"Well then, good. I think he's a great guy and very handsome."

That somehow unnerved her more. She thought it would have been something serious or dangerous. Gay was a let down. A disappointing excuse for solitude. She turned back to the vanity mirror Ruth had moved into the guest room, looked at herself firmly, avoiding the comical lighter patches under her eyes and just as she was going to call her back in, Jess opened the bedroom door and walked in, followed by the make-up artist.

"How are we doing in here?" Jess sung out grabbing Kate by both shoulders as soon as she could move Dolores away.

"Are you ready for me?" Julie the make-up artist finally edged back into her position near Kate's face.

"She is doing fine. Is this what you're wearing?"

Dolores looked over Jess' pink butterfly sleeve chiffon dress.

"You don't like it?"

"We picked it out together Mom, stop harassing her. You look beautiful Jess."

"You're going to look gorgeous. What do you think of her dress Dolores?"

"It looks like something Grandma would have worn in the fifties—right sweetheart?"

"It's brand new. Designer."

She had let her hair grow out into a warm honey blonde and it was pulled back into a tight bun. When she stood under the chuppah in her white guipure lace calf-length sheath dress, the silk gauze veil kept firm in the bun by a comb; she allowed one smile to express on her face when she finally looked up into Nate's eyes, then she pursed her Chanel Roussy pink lips before the rabbi had a chance to speak. She had made it all the way across the deck and then the lawn holding her father's hand at her side. With emboldened white satin steps, each tap brushed by freshly shaved grass, fighting the cool breeze for her veil's placement, she reached the chuppah sitting at the edge of the ocean before the dock framing the water. When her father left her at the alter, she found a surprisingly unprecedented position standing across from Nate. Johnny stood at Nate's side. Jess off to Kate's right. The small gathering looked on, seated on the lawn, enjoying the occasion and the warm winter in a hush. The rabbi spoke. Nate then smiled with aplomb before beginning his vows.

"When I imagine God...I think the most beautiful embodiment...a nebula, the sun or even possibly the most excellent human in a form of perfection. Rather, I think it's in his works that we see God, in the silhouette of the mountains at sunrise, or the massive rise and fall of an oceanic wave hitting the shores of a forest. the miles of white ice in the north met with the gorgeous electromagnetic plumes of the Aurora Borealis...And in the embrace of a family during a holiday, all dressed up, smiling bright and full of joy. I see you, and me living our lives together, forever, in beautiful harmony."

Kate added her sentiment."I did fall for you instantly, and I can't imagine being with anyone else. Always love me and hold me tight-never let me go."

A blessing by the rabbi. And so, they were joined in the harmonious quantum state of love, superposed with one another in a perpetual embrace. Two bodies continuously interacting, transferring energy and momentum as a singular unit. Married.

12

Honeymoon

Bora Bora. A week of luxury resort living in French Polynesia; a gift from George and Dolores. Barry and Ruth were allowed a greater generosity and more substantial present which they revealed before the wedding. They bought them the apartment in New York City. Outright. 209 Eighth street, right off the corner of University place, apt 5M was now Nate and Kate's for keeps. A nest. Their only responsibility was to pay the monthly maintenance. Kate's parent's gift gave them a chance to escape the confines of America's supply and demand structure to find true relaxation and ease in the resort waters of the South Pacific, where the only important products were the cocktails and meals provided by a friendly native staff.

From the sky, Bora Bora looks like a prehistoric fish, it's mouth open waiting to gobble up a floating piece of itself. On the northwest of the main island is another long thin island hovering above the fish's head like a roof drawing. On this strip are multiple resorts, each with huts, straw roofs, sitting on docks which jut out of the beach into the glowing azure water. You'd think it was paradise for certain, even if you didn't know that it was the antipode of Jerusalem on the globe. I'm mentioning this because in Paradiso, Dante with a diagram, claims that Jerusalem is just over the portal to hell and earthly paradise is located diametrically opposite. And then I think that it's possible we did that by crucifying Jesus. That we opened a gateway into hell. Not us exactly, Pontius and the high priests, but we share a burden as mankind just as we share in the glory of God. I'm still not convinced about the washing of sins; it seems like a crooked deal, at the least, being unfair to Jesus, and disregarding the concept of spiritual growth and replacing it with acquiescence of the will, individually of course and in good faith-but the belief is that if you love Christ enough, He will offer you a place in heaven, almost certainly, even if you haven't attained any certain level of understanding other than the love of Christ and His acceptance as son of God, and Lord. It's lacking evolution, in that, if we have spent billions of years evolving, we would also need to evolve our minds to achieve a higher plane or at least that's what I'm assuming- that there lies in our genetics the ability to transcend to the same plateau as Christ in heaven without having to join in his body, unless his body is actually the completeness of heaven, an energy field of its own-just as humans have a putative biofield known as Prana or Qi, Christ has a domain of his own, a realm. Can we? Can we all be risen into a heavenly state and offer a similar salvation?

Nate took a dip in the water, sinking himself until his chin touched the surface, the rest of his body distorted like in a clear blue funhouse mirror. Kate looked on from a beach chair on their private dock, sipping a colada with real patient pleasure while soaking in a gorgeous 90degree sun. Of course, she took some precaution and she coated herself in Clinique spf50 lotion, shaded by a white wide-brimmed straw hat she had purchased just for the honeymoon.

"Are you coming in?" He waved from a squatted position, droplets of wet light spraying from his arm.

"I think you should get out and put on some lotion." She beckoned him already holding the lotion bottle in her hand, and he quickly rose out of the water, climbed up to the dock that was floating, grazing the South Pacific Ocean and took his seat on the lounge chair beside her refusing to dry off.

"The water is incredible, like a bathtub."

"You said that before. Let me lotion you."

He turned his already bronzed back to her, feeling the twisting of his obliques and warmth of the sun, in anticipation of his wife's hands. She squeezed a dollop into her palm and immediately placed that hand on his shoulder blade, then moving up onto his shoulder. She began to vigorously rub his back with both hands, on his sides, massaging the ribs and love handles with the creamy lotion. When her hands reached up to his shoulders again, she pulled herself closer to his back to feel the heat radiating from his skin, all the while inspecting the way his slightly longish hair laid in small curls at the back of his neck. Then with a small bite of dread, she noticed an irregular shaped red spot on his trapezius, not angry looking, worrisome.

"What's this?"

"What's what?"

"You have a little red spot on your shoulder."

"It's a birthmark probably."

"It doesn't look like a birthmark, it's slightly irregular."

"I had it before."

"No, you didn't have this spot."

"Does it look dangerous?"

"Not dangerous, just irregular."

"Probably nothing."

"You're going to the dermatologist as soon as we get back."

"I hate going to Dr. Kim's office. He pokes and prods me looking for blackheads to clear and I tell him every time that I just need the hair pills refilled."

"This is important."

"I'll have him check it out then, but not another word until we're back home. "

"You're done."

"Cooked?"

"I'm done putting on lotion." She slid back to a more comfortable position in her chair, and he let himself lay back as well, with a sticky uneasiness he blamed on his still moist back.

"Did you know that the sun's corona is actually hotter than its surface?" he said looking out at the shimmering water.

It's as close to earthly paradise as they could get and there was not much to do in Bora Bora, other than sunbathing, eating and lovemaking, which they relished in abundance. The vacation elapsed quickly and although the following day was met with a sun worshipper's enthusiasm, Nate mostly wore a tshirt the remainder of the vacation and Kate left her chair as well, joining him for yoga and hiking at other more public parts of the resort.

The day they returned Kate insisted that Nate see Dr. Kim as soon as possible, surprising herself while on the phone with the secretary by shouting,

"It is an emergency!" when explaining that he had to have an appointment for the next day. He was squeezed in the next afternoon, and Dr. Kim made it known that he gave up his lunch to see him on such short notice.

When he returned after the appointment, Kate was already waiting, home early from her own schedule.

"What did he say?" were the first words out of her mouth.

"It's nothing."

"Thank goodness."

13

"Listen to this… 'In fiction, a utopian Metaverse may be portrayed as a new frontier where social norms and value systems can be written anew. There's also a dark side that includes sex parties and Nazi re-enactments.'"

"It's evil." Kate blurted it out without much obvious consideration and continued moving their dirty lunch plates into the dishwasher from the sink.

"It's not evil. It's the future. You love the internet."

"I love the runway shows."

"We should get VR."

"I don't need to shop for my groceries with a headset."

"But what if you could actually be in the audience of a runway show." He said this hopefully.

"Now, I'm interested... but the rest of it—the dark web and trafficking, all that stuff so alive—it's evil."

"Are you afraid you'd like cybersex?"

"Only with you." She rinsed off a dish, casually, letting herself imagine their last sexual encounter which felt more potent in retrospect.

"We should really get into this."

"You're real late sweetie."

"I'm not that late. It's just getting started. I could have a virtual reality system, headset and gloves here in two days."

"Metaverse is scary."

"I have this premonitory feeling that some alien creature has implanted us with this technology—"

"—It's all about world domination." She slid the top rack of the dishwasher closed and purposefully slammed the door of the machine before setting the cycle: quick wash.

"Exactly. They get us to create a metaverse in order to connect all our minds, suck our psyches into the program and kidnap us to some other world." His excitement was evident, like a kid before the amusement park.

"Mud huts were probably not ideal, but brick houses are good. We didn't really need skyscrapers and the computer was a glorified calculator at first. Do we need alternate realities created by a machine and some coding?" Kate tried to convince him against entering virtual reality.

"It might be the only way to arrive at those other realms. Final frontier? Complete control of our own reality...becoming godlike."

"There heeere..."

"Unless, we're already in there, in the metaverse, the other realm, a copy of our reality and we're trapped inside on loop, not realizing that the alien accomplished it's task long ago..."

"Do you want me to dress up like Gamora again?"

"...and this alien has us, our minds, psyches, our consciousnesses downloaded in this program, contained by nanotech in a small niche, no bigger than a flashstick—"

"A crystal ball hanging on the collar of some alien's kitten's neck."

"So good right. But it's possible. I think it is. It's our consciousness that they'd want—the will, life force. Our bodies are mostly water."

"Physical presence has will as well," with consternation she said this and took a seat at the counter with her unfinished cup of tea from lunch, that she hadn't poured out yet, now chilled to room temperature and darkened to a brown from the teabag she refused to remove.

"You know what I mean. You would be you-thinner or smaller or bigger, but if it's not your consciousness then it's not really you anymore."

"Why then, would we be making a metaverse reality again if we're already inside." Kate raised the teacup and took a sip, then looked at him curiously.

"Because we made the metaverse, we're trapped and then the alien who telepathically coded us with the instructions to build it, has us on loop to the moment when we realized that we're now programs and—"

"He transforms us all into butterflies..."

"—Reveals himself as our God, I was going to say. Why butterflies?"

"Butterflies are a symbol of transformation. So, you think Yahweh-Jesus is an alien?"

"I don't think they are the same, but maybe Ra or some other God who we called here…"

"Ra?" This caused a momentary confusion, and she touched her cross pendant.

"Rah-sis-boom-bah…By creating the technology, and with our need. Our bodies are nodes brought into existence on this planet with an intrinsic and determinable purpose, I think, either to bring us closer to destruction or to save us, and to save the planet. As hokey as Superman and as important as Jesus. Something agitates the electromagnetic net, a disaster or a powerful occurrence creates a pressurized system, connects to our psyches in the collective unconscious and calls out like a prayer into the eternal Om, for a being, not only a human being, to come to this reality to be born to serve that purposed need." He thought he had her.

"Jesus is a metaverse?"

"Sort of. Christians join in Him, in his body and I assume his reality becomes their reality as well, which is heaven…one of the heavens."

"And you're thinking that we want to be caught and wrapped up in some alternate reality by a powerful being? Someone who steals our minds—spirits, and keeps us like goldfish?"

"A god —a savior like Jesus... not the bad guys."

"What is he saving us from?"

"Ourselves. Holocaust. Extinction. Or the cold painful enormity of this universe's justice."

"So, then he loves us."

"Enough to steal us away or at least to play the game."

"He must need us for something. Entertainment?"

"More than that. There's right and wrong, and good and bad. Heaven and Hell. We're in some sort of spiritual training."

"Don't make it dreadful." She showed her disdain by standing, then lifting the cup and saucer and moving it to the kitchen sink where she began to rinse it clean.

"What I'm saying is not meant to be dreadful-it's pernicious not to imagine the alternatives, but we are just chatting about the Metaverse...Our spirits as extensions of our souls; learning something in the Earth domain. Growing and developing, hopefully into something better through the actualities of habit. The body is a sensory tool and the mind, it helps us regulate all our interactions. It's the mind, not the spirit, but the spirit is trying to learn something through mind and body."

"So, he'd have-has our minds? Our bodies decomposed long ago on our dead planet and we're still training." Kate pressed her pelvis against the counter, leaning back into the conversation.

"We might be alive… a split consciousness living out our days in other variations and timelines. In this timeline, we would be in the Metaverse, and we'd sort of know because of the loop that we would recognize with déjàvu."

"That's horrible. I wouldn't want to know and what would it matter if we were just programs."

"The program would just be another form, a body for the spirit to develop with, eventually we could find a more suitable form once we attained a perfection. If the aliens ever let us out."

"At least there's a way out with you."

"As simple as an upload or is it download?"

"I don't want to talk about this anymore."

"Why not?"

"You were getting holy and spiritual, then you turned back to aliens."

"I was wont of a greater purpose."

"Something greater than alien domination."

"Or maybe there's a common goal..."

"Like saving the universe from evil, but why the loop?"

"Simulation hypothesis: Endgame scenario."

14

Of course, Nate informed Kate of his big opportunity in text earlier that day, from the office. "We're movin' on up," it read on her phone screen.

"You're getting a raise?" she asked in reply.
"Not quite," he responded. "I'll tell you all about it later tonight."
By the time Nate arrived home at the New York City reasoned hour of seven o'clock, Kate was already making dinner, wearing her favorite cashmere-blend leggings with a tshirt (her off duty ensemble). She allowed for the door to shut completely, but not for Nate to remove his jacket before exclaiming, "What's the big news!?"
"They're giving me an ad. My own ad," he said

pulling an arm out of his jacket, then the other. Then he opened the entryway closet to hang his designer taupe nylon jacket on its usual hanger. She replaced the stainless steel lid on top of the fettuccini she was boiling and walked towards him, meeting him at the edge of the kitchen counter for a kiss. Then she took his hand and walked him twelve feet, past their mid-century modern teak dining table with Hargrove cushioned armchairs to the Harmony sofa a few feet away, and plopped down on the linen color basket slub, pulling him down with her onto a cushion.

"Tell me everything," she said firmly still holding his hand.

"It's just an inter-industry ad, but it's important and it's my first real shot, so I'm going to make it good—"

"Great."

"That's correct—great. They're promoting a new genetically modified potato that doesn't bruise. The previous line was known to bruise and that caused a lot of wastage. They spliced a gene from a wild variant and voilà a new spud that doesn't bruise."

"That sounds fantastic."

"It is. It took them fourteen years to get this variant just right and they're pushing it for French fries and chips. So, what we're thinking of doing for the ad is a heap of potatoes, beautiful non-bruising potatoes and then standing behind the pile a cherub-faced kid, probably a boy, real cute and tough with a black eye, eating fries from a paper cone, a clear blue sky pasted behind him."

"That sounds perfect."

"It does...doesn't it. I have to put together the mock-up before we shoot. It's easy after that."

"You know how to do this?"

"I have training in the arts...Why are you doubting me? Then I get moved up to graphic designer. If it comes out as good as we planned."

"Then we live high on the hog?"

"We continue to live modestly and plan for our future travels."

"Are we modest?"

"I think that once you get your office open and I reach art director...with some hard work, a few stylistic choices and social maneuvering, we have a chance at being amongst the New York jetset."

"Oh,Yes - the beau monde."
"We will be elite."
"We are not elitist. Don't go into your Hindu caste jive."
"I'm not talking caste. I mean successful, really successful and happy."
"We are happy."
"We definitely are."
"The pasta must be ready. Are you hungry?"
"Famished."
"Good. Wash up."

The dinner conversation included more description of the Russet potato ad, some statistics about how many potatoes are lost to bruising and a general understanding of how the potato industry works, or at least what Nate had learned from his preliminary research. The pitch was in a month to a group of Idahoan businessmen and potato farmers. Nate would not be at the meeting, but rather, it would be pitched by Jess's brother, Cal, and his work associate. It was Cal who gave Nate the opportunity. "I think you're ready," he said and handed him an older Russet Corporation brochure with the title "mashed, fried, baked," in a creamy white Helvetica bold mask over a grainy brown potato skin. "Get to it," he added. Now he had a portal to real success.

15

Every eleven years or so, the Sun's magnetic field completely flips. This means that the Sun's north and south poles switch. The cycle begins at a minimum, eventually the Sun becomes enraged, disturbed by whatever events, grand and minute, which have occurred during the eleven-year cycle in this solar system, events which didn't quite balance in the cosmic design - sunspots form on the surface of the sun, many by the time the revolutions reach the maximum phase. These sunspots incite solar flares due to their increased magnetic field, 2500 times stronger than the Earth's. Do you know the saying "To save face?" (I think it's of Asian origin). It might be the shame of our inaccurate turnings, keeping us at a distance from grace and the gracefully preordained movements of the universe, repeatedly exhibiting themselves as dark spots and blotches, a disease of incongruity, showing clearly on the Sun's face. Then with some electromagnetic swirling and fuming it creates a solar storm as powerful as an explosion of a billion megatons of TNT, presumably an alarm meant to inform us of the injustice of our actions. A coronal mass ejection — the emission of charged particles into the solar system, solar winds, we are normally protected from, bombard the magnetic field and can produce currents on the Earth's crust, with the possibility of causing catastrophic damage, at least to our human technologies. An internet apocalypse. Just as Nate typed, "daikon" into the search engine, the screen shivered and then disappeared. Nate's potato ad was so successful that he was given the higher position with a raise and another produce project: Miyazaki, a Japanese agricultural bioengineering company which produces giant daikons needed some help getting a foot into the American market. A moment after the screen went black, a couple thuds could be heard coming from Brandon's cubicle as he pounded on his hard drive. A moment later he was peaking over the cubicle partition looking down at Nate, just his head and the pointed collar of his red shirt showing above the partition.

"My screen is down. Are you getting anything?"

"It's all black," Nate responded.

A few moans followed throughout the main floor of the office echoing into a holler out of Cal's office. "Anyone know what's going on?"

Joy his personal secretary replied, "I'll call IT."

A few minutes later, the screens came back up, with a dismissive regard for the lost moments and only Nate thought to search "internet outage New York." Nothing for a few moments, then a post online showing in his notifications on his phone, "Solar flare! M8 type-radio blackout!"

"It was a solar flare!" Nate shouted out with relief. His brain waves modulated from an alert Beta back to his concentrated Gamma wave when he began to search "solar flare" online. Everything was back to normal, they all thought; on the contrary, the flare and solar ejection generated a storm of high-velocity particles, and the number of particles with ten million electron-volts of energy in the space near Earth was 10,000 times greater than normal. They were buzzing with a new verve.

"Jeff came in again today. Big reveal."

"Don't tell me about Jeff. You're not allowed-doesn't Jeff have some sort of doctor-patient privilege or something? "

"He does and that's why I made up the name Jeff and I'm not going to tell you what his real name is or what he looks like. I need to tell you more."

"You told me. Big coke head."

"The coke is the least of his worries. He finally broke down today. For two months he's been telling me about his addiction and how much he's been spending on nose candy...meanwhile he's really a broken spirit."

"Isn't that what addiction is - a broken will?"

"Not really. It's psychological and neurological.

The mind and body become addicted to the effects of the drugs as well as the actual chemistry. This one, Jeff, has been hurting since childhood."

"He's been doing drugs since childhood?"

"The drugs are recent, but it was child abuse that got him. Molestation."

"Got him?"

"His parents left him with someone who they thought was a friendly neighbor, an elderly woman with a grown son and daughter. They were mostly out and about with friends in the neighborhood, the mother, held onto Jeff after school and when his parents weren't around. Better that then latch-key kid they thought. And he was content for a while gobbling mac and cheese she'd serve him, and they would watch Wheel of Fortune if he had to stay late. Seems as if he's big on Wheel of Fortune."

"And he was molested by her? What, did she make him lick her or something? "

"Not her. Her son. He was left alone with Jeff one afternoon when the mother was grocery shopping and he got to him. The son called him into his room, presumably to watch a *Buck Rogers* episode he had taped. They watched TV for a while. It was the Andromeda episode: the space band "Andromeda" causes their youthful fans to riot when they hear them playing music-something about subliminal messaging. Remember that one? Anyway, suddenly, just as one of the bandmates started strumming out an electrical synth, the son, laid back sideways on the bed, and pulled his pants down revealing his naked sex parts. Jeff didn't know what to do, so he continued to stare at the tv, trying to avoid any eye contact with the nudity. A few moments went by and then this guy sticks his finger in his own asshole and tells Jeff to watch. Then he tells Jeff to stick his finger in his asshole."

"Jeff to stick his finger in his own asshole?"

"No. He had Jeff stick his right index finger in his, the son's asshole, I'll call him Dan."

"That's it? Jeff stuck his finger in Dan's butthole?"

"That's what he said— it turned him."

"What did it turn him into?"

"He's bisexual because of it he says and has been having sex with men since high school."

"Just because of that?"

"He dropped out of college and became a stripper at some seedy gay club, PonyBoy, met some darker sorts, found himself at a party snorting cocaine after his second night on stage and hasn't been able to stop since. He says it's the only thing that makes him happy. I think he hates it- the stripping, the drugs- he just wants to be a straight-laced guy, maybe with a wife or kids and he's trapped in this porn flick shoveling blow. "

"Is he doing porn?"

"They have a lot of sex apparently. Gay sex. Bisexual sex. It's a mixed crowd and sometimes they have tricks. The patrons ask for favors, sometimes his number."

"So, he's a prostitute."

"No, I didn't say that. It's mostly sex with his sexy stripping coworkers...and a bartender. He's been sharing tales about his sexual adventures, since the first day. I think it's interesting. Exotic dancing is a world all its own. It's like they're in some sort of sex industry commune or on a compound and that's all they do is have sex and do drugs – and dance."

"That's not that bad."

"He's miserable and blames it on the molestation. Bums him out still. The cocaine affects the reward pathways in the brain and makes him feel better, like he's doing something good and cocaine use disorders frequently co-occur with stress-related disorders. So, he's got to get out. Out of that industry and into something normal. I told him to try to go back to school or to get a job at a supermarket or something, unfortunately he needs the money as well...for the snow habit."

"You're supposed to cure him of the habit, correct?"

"I'm trying to get him into rehab for a couple weeks at least, but he's not responding just yet. Dan's white ass is still on his mind. Imprinted. He's a good-looking guy and sweet. With the right encouragement he could make it back into the mainstream."

"Sounds like you have him under control."

"He's at an eightball a week now, far from control, but he has his eye on one specific stripper who just started working from midnight till two. Adorable young kid, he says, just past eighteen, like he was a couple years ago."

"Maybe love will save him."

"Don't be sarcastic, maybe though."

"I mean it-love conquers all. *'Love conquers all things, so we too shall yield to love.'*"

"Virgil. Do you want to hear about Tanya the paranoiac?"

"I don't, but this sharing was real fun."

"Thanks for listening. I had to tell someone. "

"Me. You wanted to share this pedophilic sex and drugs story with me...that is beautiful and disturbing."

"That's right. Give me a kiss."

17

"Do you want to rent a furry suit again?" Kate asked with confidence, while moisturizing her face.

"I think we should buy one. I'm still queasy from renting the last." Nate was leaning against the headboard of the bed, using the remote to flip through channels kept on mute.

"They are dry cleaned every time."

"I don't even like vintage clothes... and us with the rubbing and kissing." He stopped on the Discover Channel.

"It was more than rubbing and kissing. I understand, though. I guess we could buy a furry suit. Bunny or teddy?"

"Teddy definitely teddy."

"I like pulling on the ears."

"Whatever, either, but not white."

"Where would we keep it. Hall closet?"

"With our winter coats?"

"Under the bed."

"Under the bed."

18

It was Late Tuesday evening, a couple hours after dinner, Nate was comfortably spread in his usual corner of the sofa, completely fixated on that week's edition of *Science Today* when Kate called out, "Do you want a tea?"

No response.

"Babe, do you want a tea?"

"Huh?"

"I'm making tea...Do you want a cup?"

"Oh, yeah, sure... a cup of tea sounds nice."

"What kind? Herbal? Chamomile?"

"Green. Do we have green?"

"No green. I'll get some tomorrow. Which one?"

"Herbal then."

Kate put the kettle on the stove and

simultaneously turned the flame on. Then with some hesitation she called out again.

"Whatcha reading tonight? Looks interesting."

"It is. It's about quantum superposition." He responded without shifting his head.

She walked out from behind the kitchen counter to a position behind Nate where she peered at his magazine, focusing on the same article. Then she began to read out loud, "'Quantum superposition is made even more perplexing by the fact that it can only occur when the particles are unobserved. Simply by observing a particle in two different quantum states you cause what is known as wave function collapse and the particle again exists in only one state or the other...'"

"Good right. Basically, it's saying that particles exist in two states at the same time and only when it is observed does it adhere to one state of being, or location... dependent upon its spin..."

"Spin?"

"Movement. Particles move in different directions, and they have spin. Their quantum state is the appropriate value to describe the state. Particle attributes. Position. Spin. Energy. It's what makes each particle different. Photon, electron, muon, lepton, fermion…There are twelve matter particles and their respective antimatter equivalents and four force carrying bosons, and the Higgs boson."

"You know this?"

"I don't know it, but I'm trying to keep track."

"Track of the movement?"

"It's incredible that these tiny creatures, thousands of times smaller than a proton, they know when they're being observed and it makes a difference in their position."

"Do you think they have a choice?"

"I couldn't answer that. Nobody knows yet, nonetheless, they are affected."

"You think they're making the best choice."

"Maybe worst. Maybe it depends on the observer. At the least it's a possibility, and then probability comes into play-that's a whole other animal with innumerable variations when the particle is part of a greater living organism - it could offer an answer to the question of predestination."

The whistle of the tea pot began to blow, with a cutting noise and Kate quickly moved away from the sofa back into the kitchen.

SLAVA KORIN

"Herbal - right?"

19

An uncomfortable silence finally found them. After years of togetherness and playful volley, the affability began to dissolve, and they were left with just the crunch of the lettuce and clink of cutlery against their plates. Nate's work was still interesting and he had already shared the details of the most recent ad earlier that evening, now a fruit, the Kumato—the brown tomato. The hottest fruit on the market, known for its firmness and sweetness, sweeter because of its Brix level, much more sucrose. His goal was to have this new heirloom tomato take the place of the traditional red tomato by advertising it simply: a single Kumato against a bright red background, above it in Pantone #19-1223 downtown brown Neue Haus Grotesk, "Why are you brown?" and below it in vivid green

#12D900, Impact regular, "I'm sweeter." Genius, right? The problem was that Nate had been pigeon-holed in the industry already; vegetables, fruit and one grain, so far. Detoured to the supermarket when what he really wanted was electronics, gadgets and technology. He remembered his first time holding a Toshiba personal cassette player and radio; a halfsies purchase which his father bought him after Nate had stuffed five thousand envelops for a real estate mailer. His father paid half and Nate's salary from stuffing paid the other half. He chose it from the dozens of other cassette players in counter display, amongst which laid the infamous Sony Walkman. The Toshiba, because It was the most compact and modern looking, unbelievably small and it split open to allow for a cassette; a normal-size cassette stuck out past the metallic silver body of the device foretelling the future of digital music and the almost magical iPod nano. Everything seemed to be going smaller as that is the goal of technology- smaller, better, faster. The only things getting bigger were high rises, scraping the skies around the planet.

All of a sudden, after a bite of a sliced Kumato, Kate reacted to the silence.

"These are good."

"They really are. It's a nice produce. The salad is really delicious Katie."

"It's just the Romaine, some red onions and the tomatoes...Kumatos."

"I think it's the dressing. Balsamic?"

"Balsamic vinaigrette."

"Really nice."

"Do you want to hear about Debbie?"

"Do I want to hear about Debbie? Who is Debbie?"

"A patient."

"I don't want to hear about your patients. We discussed this."

"This one is really interesting though; I think you'll like Debbie. Euphemistically she is an alcoholic. In the old days you'd call her a classic drunk."

"Alcoholic...I don't think we're going retrograde."

"A high school teacher with substance abuse. Alcoholism to be specific, but it could be anything really, as long as she somehow could consume it."

"You don't like her?"

"It's not that. She's hurting. The fact that she is a teacher around kids makes it harmful."

"And you told her this?"

"I explained that people with addiction who abuse any substance are also somehow endangering their loved ones and coworkers, anyone really who is in their lives."

"We drink often and sometimes too much on holidays."

"She keeps a 10ml silver flask full of Scotch in her school desk drawer and gulps down a portion in between classes."

"Fancy. Are the kids aware?"

"She thinks they are not, I'm sure that some of them are aware. It's like the scent of smoke on a smoker. Another smoker might not notice or even care but someone not intoxicated would notice and they're high school kids...And one of them caught her taking a swig. A goody-two-shoes—"

"—like you."

"Not like me, but a smarty pants, a real nerd, Debbie said, who wanted to ask a few questions about an upcoming test. Caught her elbow up, mouth to bottle and with a murmur tried to close the door without a panic. Debbie called her in, and while this girl made her soft steps towards the desk, Debbie screwed on the cap and placed the bottle back in the drawer without giving it any consideration."

"She obviously gave it some consideration."

"Enough to tell me about it. The girl must have told someone else and then there's that self-conscious radiating guilt that some addicts have."

"Maybe, the girl didn't know what the bottle was. Anyway, why are you so angry with her?"

"She doesn't even get drunk anymore, she says, it's the action of drinking — of doing some-thing repetitively. Maybe doing something some-how elicit that possesses her. Like she's on rote or on a track that keeps repeating. Something cripples her normal comprehension and redirects her to the drinking every time she attempts to find a new start. Almost every day she says."

"Is there anyone else in her life?"

"Debbie has her family, but they are some-what distant. The kids—she loves the children she teaches, but feels bad every time she takes a sip...unfortunately without the sip she can't focus on the lesson plan and just thinks about taking that sip. It's very sad."

"Scary. It's scary is what it is."

"But she lives alone, and I'm sure that aggravates the drinking, makes it more appealing as a companion."

"That one needs love too."

"It's not all about love. Some of us can get along as self-sufficient individuals. Debbie should not be alone. A close friend might help, some sort of support...it seems as if she has a process addiction that's not really about substance. She's more involved with the action of drinking."

"OCD"

"I thought that as well, but it doesn't fit into the four types of obsessive compulsion, nothing about contamination or order, no aggressive thoughts. She is somehow receiving a rewarding effect from her behavior; something scratches the itch and it's not chemical like most substance abuse."

"Sounds lonely."

"It does. I've seen her three times now, always that intimating breath of sweet liquor about her.

She's not really disturbed; just disturbed by her excessive drinking."

"First step is acceptance."

"She hasn't really accepted it because she thinks that she just drinks too much and doesn't realize that she has to stop drinking liquor completely and find her relief somewhere else."

"Love."

"Exercise. I told her to start exercising, maybe join a gym.

That'll do it. Maybe she could carry her flask in a fanny pack while she does the elliptical."

"Not funny. And group. I told her to get to group and make some friends."

Nate reached for his half-filled glass of Beaujolais, wrapped his hand lightly at its base and raised it in the air. "To friends." And then he took a hearty gulp.

"Have you spoken to Johnny lately?"

20

It was an early morning for Kate. She had a meeting with her co-workers, counselors and other psychologists at the practice; something about better conviviality in the office. Nate was still asleep when she left the apartment. She left a note and neglected a goodbye kiss.

"If you're just reading this note, you've slept too late. I left some bacon in the Rubbermaid container near the stove —enjoy, but remember to do your steps and get your act together."

Kate who focused on excellence (sometimes confused with success), had a way of nudging Nate out of his privileged adolescent disposition with reverse psychology and mild control, which never really worked.

21

The Christmas party at Nate's work ran late, later than he and Kate had expected. It was a good time, if anything. The Primum execs rented out a nearby restaurant, a Brazilian steakhouse, called Fogo, a favorite amongst the staff who stayed late and wanted to avoid eating alone or finishing leftovers of a family meal they had missed. The food was too heavy for lunch, and who can eat so much meat in one sitting, flame-broiled, served on long metal skewers at the table, each hunk of meat made to slide down the metal spear obediently, piece after piece until the patron calls for a halt. They didn't serve the regular portions at the holiday party; they had everything done in hor-de-œuvre size, carried around on gleaming silver trays. Tiny Pincanha sandwiches, bacon-wrapped tenderloin, and these delicious slivers of churrasco served with a dollop of salsa verde. They had a new client, for the new year, a meat wholesaler named Weischler, that wanted special attention and offered to flip the bill for this celebratory event, at the same time letting the staff, who would be working on the campaign for the better part of the following year, to have a taste of the meats they sold and wanted promoted. The meat was very good, succulent even, but by ten PM, the staff and their escorts were full up, stuffed and drunk on the best whiskey and vodka there was to offer a crowd of influencers. Their sharp designer and bridge suits crumpled and the women, so fit and in form at the beginning of the event were already bending their ankles and letting themselves breathe by the time Cal came out with a white beard and red Santa hat on, ready to gift the raffle ticket holders, one ticket for each couple; yellow paper tickets with serial numbers they received upon entering the restaurant. 98782 was the number on the ticket Nate handed Kate, to hold in her clutch until the time came and she pulled it out as soon as Cal shouted, "It's time everybody! Let the holiday spirit consume you.

Santa, me, I am ready give out your Christmas gifts," he said this loudly, garbled because he had drank too much to contain himself and found it pleasing to shout into the crowd of employees who really were in no position to judge him; he had made partner earlier that year and it seemed as if all fear and insecurity deserted him at that point of achievement. "Who's been naughty and who's been nice? Who cares? You're getting a gift anyway. Let's see here..." Cal pulled a ticket out of a different Santa hat his secretary, Joy, was holding, standing next to him in a green elf hat and a very pretty Asian-inspired red satin sheath. "First prize-present goes to 98760!" Every head in the crowd dipped in unison to look at their tickets. A few so bleary eyed, they had to raise the piece of paper up, holding it in front of their faces trying to figure out if they had the winning ticket. Cal waited for a moment. "Anyone with the winning ticket?" "I have it!" A short portly man with black-rimmed glasses called out from the left corner, near the bar, Marc, a copy editor with the agency, known for late hours and the tuna fish sandwiches he sometimes left in the refrigerator of the employee lunchroom.

"Marc has the winning ticket everybody!" They cheered together as Marc walked to the front of the room, where Cal was standing on a raised platform, where there usually was a buffet table, in front of a stack of at least twenty wrapped boxes sitting on a red cloth-covered table; Joy clenching the velvety red ticket-holding hat next to him and smiling with excitement. "Come on up!" Cal took one red paper foil wrapped box from the stacked pile and handed it to Marc as soon as he was close enough. "Show us what you got!" Kenny, an assistant, shouted from the back of the gathering. Marc took to opening the present, tearing the wrapping paper off in fast noisy rips. Before it was all off, he could see the gift. It was an android phone, the BorgX in a chrome box. A model for which the agency had created a campaign at the beginning of the year. A successful ad featuring a silver metal cyborg in combat, red lasers flying by and explosions behind him; a moment later a frame with the same cyborg resting on top of a heap of black clad robots, the enemies kaput, stacked under him. BorgX rings with a synthesized pulsing sound and our hero, the cyborg answers in a British voice, "So, glad you called. I'm just finishing up." Just then one of the enemy robots' beeps under him and he gives it a kick. They ran the spot in mostly English-speaking countries, and it did well in Germany. Nate and Kate won a phone as well. The elaborate box which included a charging stand and head-phones wouldn't fit in her clutch or in either of their coat pockets, so it sat in Nate's lap the whole cab ride home, until he tossed it onto the sofa upon arriving at the apartment at almost 1AM. They were exhausted, barely able to take their clothes off and found the bed in a stupor, they collapsed onto it, with Kate's dress unzipped, and Nate who only managed to get his pants off, laid back with his arms outstretched. He fell asleep al-most immediately. Something about drunkenness imposes a guilt when there are two people in bed, who are in a couple, and who would normally be attracted to one another; as if the inebriation is just cause for sex, no matter the level of drunkedness, as long as both persons are enough awake (assum-ing they still like one another) to engage in sexual activity—it is somehow required. This is how Kate felt and after the first fifteen-minute doze with her face pressed into the mattress almost reaching the pillow, she woke and reached for Nate's appendage with whatever vigor she had left. He was still clothed in the white, blue-striped boxer shorts and his best white button-down shirt, the armpits sweated through. She bent at the waist and called his name, "Nate?" Something slurred came out of his mouth and faded with a breath. "Nate." She lifted her arm and finally placed her right hand on his flaccid member and squeezed. Nothing. She squeezed again with more affection pulling herself closer until her head touched his hip, she couldn't move any further and fell asleep again with her hair covering her face and her hand resting on him.

The next morning Nate woke at the mercifully later winter sunrise time of 7:20AM, because the sun was burning bright through their bedroom window. They hadn't managed to close the drapes the night before and the light woke him to the dull pain behind his eyes, as if the liquor had dried out his brains. Kate's hand still on his groin. After a moment of roused confusion, he tried to lift himself up to a seated position, sliding Kate's hand off of him. "Were you going to take advantage of me, Kate?" he mumbled as best as he could.

22

A quiet Tuesday evening, a couple hours after a tastefully mild dinner, Nate was reading something in the living room and Kate, she had the task of unloading the dishwasher, a task she agreed to because Nate had rinsed and loaded the dishes. By the time she began to unload the bottom shelf with the plates from which they ate veal scallopini, and the pot which just a short while ago boiled some angel hair pasta as a contorno with garlic and oil, she could smell the odor emanating from the trash container at the other end of the single line kitchen. Garbage that had not been emptied since Saturday night and contained the chicken carcass she refused to make soup out of, from Sunday evening's dinner, along with Monday evening's unfinished Chow Mein.

"The garbage honey. Our chicken from Sunday is having a second life in there. Why can't you take out the garbage regularly?"

"I'm capable."

"Then why don't you?"

"I'm busy at the moment."

"You're always busy with something superfluous."

"Above your head?"

"Not above my head pompous asshole, it's all just at nose level. Can't you smell it?"

"I'm studying."

"Studying to smell reality. There are more than just smarts and academics. We're in the real world and it stinks."

"I know you're fighting down there in the trenches, but us philosophers are having a hard time keeping our wits about us up here in the clouds."

"I understand honey, you're full of shit and we're surrounded by it."

"Something like that."

"By the way. Do we have any of that silver lining left?"

23

Things were going smoothly. Nate was doing well at work and Kate found some of her own success, they now wanted to try a night apart, not as an experiment, as a matter of necessity; there was an addiction convention to attend up in Poughkeepsie. A few hundred psychologists were gathering to discuss addiction in the new millennium. A little late as it was already 2011, however, a noble effort. They were concerned with the affects of Benzedrine in the fifties, marijuana in the sixties, heroin in the seventies, cocaine in the eighties, ecstasy in the nineties and alcohol throughout the century. How has our abuse of substances affected our movement into the 21st century? Are we wiser and fuller with experiences or dumbed by chemical abrasion and weaker as a society because of our addictions? Kate took the train up that Friday afternoon, hoping to focus her attention on some research. It was decided that Nate would remain in the city, to expect the electrician because there was a problem with the recessed lighting in the living room. They wouldn't dim correctly. Maintenance was to arrive Saturday afternoon to give it a look and that would mean, possibly not enough time for the two of them to return from the conference and although Nate didn't mind, he fussed about it at work anyway, sharing the Friday night detail with Brandon, possibly expecting sympathy.

"Kate's out of town tonight."

"Oh really?" Brandon was interested.

"She's got a conference upstate."

"Worried about being alone-are you?"

"Not worried. It's just the first time."

"Well, you're a big boy now."

"Thanks for the encouragement."

"Would you like to join me? I am going to the Cubby Hole to partake in some drinking and debauchery. It's a really mellow crowd and we'd love to have a straighty..."

"You didn't hear about the night I tongued my roommate in college on ecstasy."

"Everybody made out with their college roommate. Come along. Join us."

"Are you a cult?"

"Not quite, but we know how to have a good time. You know a few of them already."

"I think it could be fun."

It turned out to be more amusing than he had expected, a night of licentiousness with a crowd just as familiar with social constraints, finding time to unwind with a few laughs and a couple drinks, this group was unwilling to inhibit themselves for the satisfaction of anyone else. Brandon, a pack leader, invited Nate suspecting something liberal about him and although not at first, an ulterior motive developed within the warmth of the bar, because of the heat of the liquor in their bellies and heads, and the compromising joviality of roistering.

When the lesbian bartender with the shaved head and bullring nose piercing asked, "Who's your new friend?" Brandon responded, "This is my coworker, Nate. Isn't he beautiful?"

"I thought you found a new one already."

"I don't want to talk about that. Tonight...is special, Nate's first time home alone and if I'm correct... first time at a gay bar. Am I correct?"

"You are...my first time."

"We'll have to make it special," Sadie coaxed him.

"Just do what I do, and you'll be fine. Two whiskey sours, please Sadie."

"Coming right up." Sadie reached for the whiskey and pulled a plastic bottle with sour juice mix from below the bar.

Brandon began to tap on the bar top with both hands, flapping them against the molded wooden bar rail like a seal.

"Are you nervous?"

Sadie had already poured the whiskey, juice and ice, and began to shake the stainless-steel shaker.

"Why would I be nervous?"

Brandon's arm shot out and wrapped around Nate's shoulder. "I'm happy that you're here."

She poured the cocktail into two tumblers which she placed in front of them.

"I think I'm happy about it as well."

Just then Sadie finished the drinks with maraschino cherries, dropping them from the stems into the orange-colored liquid with a tiny plop.

"Here are your drinks, boys."

"Thanks so much Sadie." Brandon lifted one tumbler and handed it to Nate, then lifted his own and said, "Cheers! To nights off."

Nate repeated, "Cheers." A light clink and two big gulps. The music became louder, Cher's voice ringing out, "If I Could Turn Back Time," she sang, pouring her meaty, bright, contralto voice out through the overhead speakers of the bar. A bar with real character, rainbow flags hanging on strands from the ceiling, visible in the distant mirrored back wall. Mirrored just above chestnut wainscotting, a few tables underneath it and ban-quettes at one side of the small dance floor with an electronic mirror ball simulator hanging above, flashing streams of green, yellow, red lights on the walls and floor, speckling faces with oblong circles of light.

"The rest of the gang will be here soon. So don't you worry."

"Why would I worry?"

"I just wouldn't want you to think that you're

stuck with just me all night long...it's a lively crowd."

"I can see that. Nate scanned the room, looking over a modest group of people, presumably lesbians and gays in denim and plaid, tight t-shirts with humorous slogans and interesting androgynous haircuts. They moved about the room, mingling with exaggerated affection and meaningful affectations meant to keep outsiders away. Only those who got it could imagine a life like this, no different than anyone else except your only about six percent and God might disapprove of your love, leaving you to the devil who as we know is also judgmental and prejudiced in a meaner way...and really, it's just sex, they think – except, without true love is any of it worth the hassle? All that dancing and drinking late into life, seems a disavowal of the more conservatively scheduled mainstream, and at the same time, completely a result of popular culture which nurtured androgyny in fashion and music, starting as early as the twenties when bobbed flappers danced enthusiastically, and finally went full steam in the sixties, when men began to grow their hair long again and women wanted to wear their boyfriend's jeans, confusing the modern moment and making way for millennial generations freed from convention, tuning society to equality. Nate looked on unnecessarily superimposing himself into the crowd, looking for a position he could fill amongst them, trying to catch phrases, glances, something that would tell him either way who he was to these people. Not regular folk, common for New York City though, more imposing as a constituency in a grouping and evidently more joyful in celebration. For some, less offensive in this, their playful setting than at those civil rights rallies. But it's the new millennium and we have gay marriage, so why should a little flair cause a ruckus.

"There's Cal! Cal! Over here!"

Cal squeezed through the crowd making his way over to the bar where Nate and Brandon were standing together.

"You're not supposed to be here," Cal immediately said to Nate with consternation.

"Don't fret. I'll put him back safe and sound." Brandon smiled with his remaining boyish sweetness.

"Kate's out of town. I didn't know you were gay."

"Still am gay. What are you two drinking?"

"Whiskey sour this evening. You should try one."

"I'll have a beer, Sadie. The Czech." Cal motioned to Sadie.

"You got it, Cal."

"Does she know everyone?"

"We're regulars."

"You're here every Friday?" Nate seemed disappointed.

"Almost. Sometimes a club. Why is that strange somehow. It's our watering hole."

"I just don't remember the last time I went out."

"Let's see how this goes." Brandon clinked Nate's glass again, with more intention, and then he clinked Cal's beer bottle, just before Joy showed up, bouncing out of the crowd of revelers in a tiny black dress.

"Nate! I can't believe you're here with us! What a treat." She kissed his cheek quickly.

* * *

"Where are you?" Nate could hear the worry in Kate's voice.

"I'm still in bed honey. How's the conference going?"

"The conference ended yesterday evening, late. I'm standing in our living room. You're not in the bed or in the apartment. Where are you?"

"I'm at Brandon's still."

"Why would you be at Brandon's —in bed?"

"We got blitzed last night and came back to his place. I couldn't make it downtown alone."

"You were so drunk—"

"—And high," he added.

"—That you couldn't take a cab a distance of thirty blocks to sleep in our bed?"

"I'll be there in twenty minutes."

"Did you have sex with Brandon, Nate?"

Hardly a breath.

"Nate?"

"Kate, I'm going to be home in just a moment."

Last night's odor hung all around Nate in a sour fuzzy burn that hurt more than his headache, a reminder of the third whiskey sour he had which he shouldn't have had and then mixed with the inhalations of one of Brandon's quickly rolled green crack marijuana joints, a reference to kryptonite and to the wakeful buzz it's supposed incite. It definitely caused a buzz and did weaken the strength of at least one man who in his intoxication kissed a boy again. And again, until they were naked on Brandon's bed engaging in the act of foreplay, and surprised by their attraction for one another. Seems as if the friendliness at the office developed into something more, but not really more than just a romp as was made obvious when Nate slapped Brandon's ass before leaving, hollering out, "See you at the office Monday." Brandon responded with a holler as well, "Can't wait, lover." By the time the cab was halfway to his apartment, Nate noticed that the cabdriver's finished bacon, egg and cheese breakfast sandwich was still competing for attention in the cabin with his own now embarrassing scent. Kate would be upset, most definitely upset with the scent and last night's events. After exiting the cab, he hurried upstairs, as fast as the elevator could lift him, pausing only to greet his surprised doorman. When he finally opened the front door, Kate was standing at the kitchen counter staring out the window at the windows of the building across the street, barely conscious of his entrance, preoccupied with something closer to the meaning of life, or rather it's purpose.

"Kate," he said, "Don't overreact, please."

"It's not a big deal. I'll just get used to the fact that you're a cocksucker."

"I thought you liked gays."

"I'm very gay-friendly except for when some fairy tries to swoop up my man—You are not gay."

"I know I'm not."

"Then why did you have sex with a guy?"

"I'm not sure."

"Did you suck his dick?"

"I didn't."

"You're lying! Everyman wants to suck his own dick, so why wouldn't suck your boyfriend's dick."

"He's not my boyfriend."

"He's your work-boyfriend. Are going to sneak kisses at work now? My god—have you been doing that? Have you been flirting all this time at the office like two school kids?"

"Not really, but we get along."

"You freak'n get along! I understand that you get along. I can't believe it... I was at the Christmas party. We were introduced. He kissed my cheek. Does anyone else know?"

"No, no one else knows... how could someone know already... we just woke up...unless, he told somebody... but why would he?"

"Cause he's fucking evil!"

Then the cordiality ceased, and she began to only yell in whaling moans and garbled hateful words. He couldn't shift his glance from the penumbra cast by the glass bowl filled with apples and oranges sitting on the kitchen counter. The cylindrical form filled with the colored spheres in green and orange would not let him face her or even look in her direction while she berated him and eventually began cry. There was nothing else in the world that moment except for the apples and oranges in that bowl and her screeching. He couldn't imagine that his actions would do this to her. The crying continued, causing some vibrating tension throughout the apartment, tension which Nate was unwilling to consider at that moment as he was on the verge of some sort of discovery, a new facet to his self that was blubbering as well, calling out for recognition.

"I'm leaving. I don't know if you care or not."

Kate stopped her sobbing with a sniffle. "Permanently? Where are you going?"

"I need some space."

"I didn't tell you to leave."

"I'm going to clear my head."

"I'm the one who's been betrayed."

"I know. I have a lot to think about as well."

Nate closed the front door behind him with some disappointment and walked away from her broken sobs. In the elevator he decided on a direction and after a few steps in the brisk autumn weather he found the B train subway station at Broadway and Houston. Descended underground and jumped on a train headed south towards the beach. People on and off along the route, finding their homes and shops in various neighborhoods. Exiting in clumps from the sliding metal doors as if they all knew one another. The personality of their neighborhoods visible on their faces and clothing they wore. Nate sat alone peeking at them and peering out the windows to catch glimpses of rooftops and signage as the train made the ten-mile, forty-five-minute ride, down to its last stop, Brighton Beach. The doors slid open for him, and he could immediately smell the ocean just two blocks away. A few minutes later he sat on a bench across from the Atlantic Ocean again; a few hundred feet of sand between him and 3.8 billion years of constant churning movement and stasis existing solely because of the ocean's enormity. *We need to be bigger.* The sun perched higher than normal that Saturday morning shone a cool light glowing in its own pool of crisp blue. There was a paucity of birds that day and he only really noticed the two seagulls which were flying above him, together like double-sided knives spinning in unison. Diverted from their dance, by a ringing squawk he returned his stare towards the water as it poured onto the sand drawing a wetted outline of itself. *We need to define ourselves.* He thought about his marriage and couldn't muster any guilt; simply, it felt less powerful now. The union, the commitment that he had made had become loosened by his immorality; in danger of becoming untethered. Adultery, he thought, how disgraceful. But he knew that he still loved Kate. He could feel it, now more than ever. *We must move past this.*

For a moment he imagined being gay and it left a sweet and sour flavor in his mind that chilled him with some excitement. It wasn't quite right for him. Kate was right for him. It was decided by the sun and the moon and the stars. He breathed in and out allowing the salty air to cleanse him, repeatedly in and out, in and out with full contented breaths until there was only Kate again. An hour passed and lifted himself up and he left, back onto the train where there was now a huddle of winsome riders on their way to the city. Some exited in northern Brooklyn, most waited to reach Canal Street, choosing an excursion in the clamor of Chinatown or the village. Others waited for Nate to get off at the same station from where he began his trip.

Kate was in the kitchen when he entered, fussing about with the kettle trying to make tea. It seemed the most difficult thing to do at that moment, at least she had stopped crying and only the streaks of her tears and reddish skin hollered cheater at Nate when he faced her again. Nothing was said until he removed his jacket and hung it in the closet. Then he turned to her and said in a sanguine manner, "We're staying together. There's no question about that."

"We are. I decided the same."

"Nothing has really changed between us. It was just a foolish mistake. I was inebriated."

The kettle sang out, a screaming whistle that burned through their conversation. Kate moved with some regained finesse to lift the kettle from the right burner of the stovetop and placed it on the left burner, turning off the flame at the same time with her other hand. Then she waited for all the noise to settle.

"I'm thinking that as well, but I think we need therapy. Couples therapy."

"I don't know if that's necessary. I think we have a handle on this," he uttered calmly attempting not to rankle the composure of the room.

"Just hear me out. You let someone into this relationship, and I need to let someone in, to balance the equation...someone who can help us."

"Brandon is not in this relationship."

"Anymore."

"Do this for me so that we can be completely honest."

"I'm more likely to be honest without a proctor."

"Give this a chance. I believe in therapy."

Kate walked over to Nate and let her hand fall on his chest. She could feel the chill of the outside air on his sweater and smell a faint wispy scent of the ocean still around him.

"If it means that much to you then let's try it, but please understand that I'm fine."

"I'm not, and this will help. Would you like a cup of tea?"

There was only the evening left to that day, most of it they spent apart. They slept together in the same bed regardless, somehow fearful of an improper caress, as if they had already been apart for years.

It was the following morning when Nate opened the front door to pick up his Sunday paper that he found Brandon lying against the wall in the hallway just outside the doorway.

"Good morning, Brandon," Nate said in a sturdy morning voice.

Brandon instantly woke and opened his eyes, clumsily standing himself up upright before saying, "I have to explain to your wife. I feel horrible."

"I don't think that's a good idea."

"I came here right after Splash. I got wasted, but I couldn't sleep knowing that I caused you two to fight and I made it all the way here and fell asleep at the foot of your door. Is she here?"

"How did you get into the building?"

"Kate?"

"It's not necessary. Really. We'll work it out."

"Is that Brandon? Are you fucking kidding me? Are you dating now?" Kate came raging out of the bedroom towards the front door.

"Just hear me out Kate. I need you to understand because I really feel horrible." Brandon walked past Nate into the living room just far enough away from Kate.

"There's nothing to understand." She stops before getting too close without a real motive for the momentum.

"Really, just please give me a minute. I didn't mean to beleaguer you or Nate—it was completely selfish, mostly without strategy. It just happened. Two guys hanging out. It's normal in the gay world."

"Is it really?" Kate looked over at Nate.

"I wouldn't know."

"Are you trying to find out?"

"I'm trying to keep us together and to avoid a cataclysmic event."

"Do you think the Earth is going to stop spinning because you decided that you want to suck dick."

"We just got close, over the months."

"Over the months? Has this happened before?"

"Listen, I didn't mean to sully anything here between the two of you..."

"No, nothing happened before."

"You didn't mean to sully-you smarmy faggot."

"Hey there, sister..."

"There you go again. We said we weren't going to use that word."

"Pardon my candor. I'm the one who was betrayed."

"It was meaningless!"

"Playful. I don't think it was meaningless," Brandon countered.

"Do you see a future with my husband?"

"No, but it wasn't meaningless."

"Are you two bonkers? I was high. We fooled around. It's stupid."

"You can't work with him anymore."

"What do you mean I can't work with him any-more—I don't have another offer at the moment and I'm making headway."

"I gave him head. Is that what you want to hear?"

"Not from you. I want you, Nate, to tell me everything after our interloper leaves."

"I'm not leaving until I have my say. We're all adults, children of a new millennium and it's time we understood one another. I was desperate-in pain. I just broke up with my boyfriend earlier this year and Nate really is the sweetest and we got to drinking and he looked so delicious. I couldn't control myself."

"That's not a good excuse."

"Kevin left me a month after we moved in together. We had been dating for the better part of the past year, and then I farted or something and he left. I wanted more and sometimes you miss the supposed to have been more than what you actually had, because you hardly had anything, nothing really, just a supposed interaction. It's like fate promised me something and delivered only on the coincidence, leaving me wanting the actualization of the fantasy, a blue balls occurrence in time and space, a lackluster blow from a fairy's kiss, none of the glittering magic."

"And you decided to snatch my man?"

"I was obsessed with Kevin. You have to understand."

"He didn't snatch me."

"I'm not talking to you right now."

"I tried to get Kevin back, but he wouldn't even respond to my texts, not last week and not Friday night when I was out with Nathan."

"And you lunged at my husband?"

"Not intentionally. It was instinct. Can you try to understand me?"

"If you were a patient I would try but, I have no reason or desire to understand you after what you did."

"Please…"

"Get out."

"Thanks for explaining Brandon," Nate tried to disarm the situation.

"You're welcome, Nathan. I really want you two to stick together."

"I'm sure you do."

"See you at work."

Brandon found his way to the door and exited with a finalizing, "Goodbye then."

"Definitely therapy—this week. You have no choice in the matter."

25

The Monday after the cosmic collapse in some far off part of the galaxy, a star inverting into a black hole or something, Kate contacted her friend Sheryl from graduate school. Dr.Sheryl Feinman was working as a marriage therapist in a small practice uptown. They had only been casual friends and Kate really never had much shame. This event was not going to smirch her either. The call lasted only a few minutes, but she was able to explain briefly that her marriage was in trouble and she and her husband needed counseling. Would you, Sheryl? Of course, she replied and an appointment for that Friday at 6PM was scheduled. They would have to last at least the five-day week together.

Nate immediately realized that his indiscretion with Brandon was a mistake upon returning to his desk that Monday. On the letter B of his keyboard laid a silver foil wrapped Hershey's chocolate kiss. When Nate let out a breathy sigh, Brandon called out from behind his cubicle.

"Lover, you've come back!"

"None of that please. I don't think I could take it."

"Well, whatever. I was just being frisky."

"Then we have an understanding."

"Most definitely. No flirting in the office you mean. How's the wifey?"

"She's calmed down some."

"It was really no big deal."

"Seems as it was. Let's not talk about it anymore."

With that Brandon rolled back into the confines of his cubicle, then he hollered out, "But we're doing lunch right...at Singapore House?"

"Lunch at Singapore House."

"And we share a plate of fried taro."

"Why not."

Lunch was easier than expected because Cal, and Cathy, Brandon's supervisor joined our lunch date, silencing most of his intended conversation.

The remainder of the day buzzed along quickly. Tuesday was serene. Wednesday, Brandon mentioned Nate's trim physique in the employee lounge and combined it with a congratulatory, "You were really good." This comment unfortunately titillated Nate in a most amusing way, awarding him some conceit and leaving him as confused as when Johnny tickled his ear at the dance. Nothing on Thursday. Then Friday at approximately 4PM, Brandon asked, "Any plans tonight?" To which Nate responded in a self-possessed manner, "We have a couples therapy session this evening." Expressing the bite with each word.

That Friday just past 6PM Nate and Kate made themselves as comfortable as possible in Sheryl's office, seated together on her loveseat sofa with her looking on from her tan nubby armchair. They were early, arriving directly from their offices, still buzzing from the day's other appointments and labor. Nate somewhat bewildered by the chain reaction, while Kate with an imposing composure belied her actual thoughts, evident in small gestures: her clenched hands and the tight posture she kept, her knees together, unlike her usual position with crossed legs. We'll get through this was her encouragement. Nate on the other hand expressed: how the hell did this happen? In expectation of an uncomfortable repartee, they sat as close as they could get without touching and avoided eye contact until Sheryl tapped on her notebook with the tail end of her pen.

"Let's find out what the problem is here. Kate briefed me already. Who wants to go first?"

"Then I'll continue… it's been only a few days. I've been imagining Nate…" She turned her head to face Nate while still avoiding his eyes, "…with Brandon…or some other guy."

"That's not so strange after something like this."

"Nonsense." He was visibly abashed.

"I've actually begun to check out random attractive men on the street and I think that one would look good with him-in a relationship…and it hurts because I displace myself from our equation. Then I think, just keep him close. It was only one time. He's a straggler. That's all it is–you have to keep him close." Turns to Nate again. "I'd shove you up my asshole and walk about if I could, but that would make both of us uncomfortable and

I'm all out of hoop skirts, Babe." She flopped her hands in front of her as if lifting an imaginary skirt with dismay.

"You'd want to hide me under your skirt to keep me straight?"

"Up my ass to keep you from wandering."

"I'm not wandering. It was a mistake. Whiskey sour and green crack is a bad combination turns out." His complexion began to turn pallid.

"You still think that it's funny."

"I'm concerned that you don't think that me fooling around with some guy high on booze and pot one night, while you're at an addicts' convention, is most certainly hilarious." Then his blood pressure rose again to redden his cheeks.

"Addiction therapy convention. And it was Brandon from work who you share a cubbyhole with, not some random guy. How was he this week-chipper?"

"We haven't spoken much since Sunday. There's some tension." His face finally found a nice hued pink, with the brighter warmth of dilated capillaries on his cheeks.

"No-hey there! Friday was fun-How about do-ing it again sometime? He sits right next to you."

"Just office talk."

"Like pass me the tape dispenser? Don't Tim's pants look extra snug today?"

"Who's Tim?" He turned abruptly to face her.

"I don't know what other gays you work with." She continued to look directly at Sheryl with concentration.

"Let's think this out for a minute. You're up-set that this happened with this Brandon whom Nate works with? Would you care less if it was a stranger?" Sheryl crossed her plump thighs into a cross legged position which left her designer heeled right foot pointing out humorously, as she became more consumed by the conversation.

"I'd probably care more, because Brandon, I thought was a nice guy."

"And you said he was very attractive."

"I didn't say to fuck him." Kate said this loudly turning her head swiftly to face Nate's reddened left ear.

"Hold on. Did you know that Nate has homo-sexual tendencies?"

"That's going too far. I don't have tendencies. I have loving non-discriminating moments."

"He told me about his college roommate. They fooled around apparently."

"That changes the dynamic." Sheryl uncrossed her legs and leaned forward slightly, pinching the edge of her notebook laying in her lap with her midsection's soft roll of excess fat.

"Nate you might be missing something in this relationship that you somehow need to develop. You have a desire for same-sex affection."

"Don't we all have a desire for same sex affection?" Nate propped his elbow up on the armrest and leaned his head against his hand with the consolation.

"More than affection. I mean that when you're uninhibited you enjoy sexual experiences with men."

"Just twice."

"He's not gay. Tell her." Kate said this to Sheryl without the need to look at Nate.

"I'm not gay."

"I'm not saying that you're gay, however, you're not completely straight neither. Research has discovered that human sexuality lies on a scale from 1 to 6. One being the straightest and six being the gayest. Your probably not a six, but it also seems like you're not a one."

"We watched *Kinsey*."

"We love each other. We're perfect together."

"There is something missing." Sheryl leaned back into her chair with a breathless sigh.

"Nothing is missing. I was just high."

"And when you're at your loveliest you desire men."

"I'm open to their affection, sometimes."

"Are you some kind of loose booze whore? What do you mean you're open to their affection? How many men have you been open to?"

"Just the two."

"Two might be enough. I think you two need to decide what you want to do. The healthy thing would be to explore each of your desires to see what makes you happy."

"We're not that healthy and besides this one night stand we're happy."

"Then I suggest we work on keeping you two

together. I'd like the both of you to start thinking about forgiveness."

"What would he have to forgive me for?" This she said looking intently at Nate with concern.

"You knew about his predilection and confronted him improperly."

"I called him one morning and found out that he was still in his boyfriend's bed."

"You have to let it go. It's not about him being with a male or a female-it's the adultery that's the issue. He turned to someone else."

"I didn't turn."

"You found sexual pleasure from someone other than your partner."

"This is so obtuse... but I understand that I'm the one at fault." Nate became disheartened.

"Good."

"See, Babe, not that hard."

"I told you I was sorry."

"No, you didn't."

"I apologize for cheating... it was completely impromptu. Will never happen again."

"That's what I wanted to hear." Kate found a remaining note of victory and with that she smacked him on the thigh and turned to smile at Sheryl the therapist.

"You're not going to that job anymore."

26

It was a spur of the moment decision; the romantic getaway was intended to calm the uncomfortable domestic disturbance. Something they decided upon Friday evening just after the session with Dr.Sheryl. The healing would begin as soon as possible with a spontaneous trip upstate to the small town of Beacon. They reserved a room at a bed&breakfast called the Swann Lake Inn and anticipated visiting the modern museum situated within its borders, hiking the nearby Mt.Beacon and eating at their favorite Middle Eastern restaurant, as quaint as the town. Saturday morning the doorman had their car brought out to the front of the building from the garage and Kate took the driver's seat for the hour and a half long drive up. FDR drive north to I-87, then further onto the Sprain Brook Parkway, NY-9A, off onto Briarcliff-Peekskill Parkway, then US-6. Beacon sits off of NY-9D at the side of the Hudson River on a hilltop. The trees were not turning, nor was it glorious springtime. It was the beginning of summer. The hot of the season had filled the air, almost everything had bloomed already and only the hottest months of July and August were left to endure. Being from Miami, Nate and Kate were completely accustomed to the heat. They didn't expect the convection of their tempers, from troubled to impassioned. The fervor of there pheromones could be felt tangibly in the car ride up, their words almost breathy and excited. Kate offered sharp glances, peeking at Nate every now and again while she drove. Nate fixated on the side of the road, looking out the window with long purposeful gazes.

"I want this heat to let up a little. It's so hot today...we should have come up next month."

"It's almost apple-picking season...in September. We can visit then," Nate said.

"When have you ever gone apple-picking in your life?"

"There's an apple orchard near Beacon, in Fishkill. I came across it while researching the produce we farm up here," less timidly.

"Are you finally a farmer."

Kate reached for the frosty snowflake button on the climate control section of the car's dashboard and depressed it, urging the air conditioning system to manipulate the refrigerant, changing it from a liquid to a gaseous state, whereby it absorbs the heat from the air and then propels it through the vents in the dashboard, cooling the cabin of the car down to a more pleasant 68degrees. Nate had control of the sound system, keeping his cellphone, plugged into the car stereo's auxiliary input jack, tucked at the side of his thigh.

"Can you forward to next one? I can't stand this song when it gets roaring...sounds like some sort of monstrous machine," Kate said without looking at him.

"I like this one.'"

"Just please." She turned quickly to face him,

Nate lifted the iPod and found the song Kate requested, placing the aluminum and polycarbonate plastic multi-purpose computer back in the crevice between his leg and the seat.

"That's much better. This is such a beautiful song," Kate cooed with enthusiasm at the first aching synthy violin sounds.

"The video is really well-designed."

"State-of-the-art," he added a little.

"...with the white plastic robots making love. It's really something."

"Lexan polycarbonate," added some more.

"What?"

"The robot shells are made from a polycarbonate called Lexan, it's a thermoplastic developed in Germany a while back, virtually unbreakable."

"How did you know that? *Science Today* again?" she questioned him with a note of disdain.

"There was a making of documentary, I saw online at work one day."

"Must have been a busy day at the Prime Meats Bath House." Then she broke; Nate let it slide by him without much notice.

"I'm happy that we're taking this weekend to be with each other and you were correct about Brandon. He's been a little flirty this week. I'm thinking of finding another position, maybe at Garland White or Cooper, Sterling, Hamm," Nate conceded, hoping that this information would alleviate some concern.

"That's not a bad idea and I know you don't want to hear this right now... I'm thinking that we should move back to Miami. Sell the apartment and just move back down." Kate began to look at Nate sporadically turning her head like a sprinkler, looking from the road, at him, and back again repeatedly.

"Hold on. That's too drastic. Once we're apart, there won't be anymore tension."

"Once you and Brandon are apart? I feel like you're not telling me something."

"I just don't think I can work there anymore."

"Well, good. Would you be able to find work in Miami?"

"All the agencies are up North. I don't want to leave the city."

"Just think about it. I think it's important that we really try."

"I'm trying. We're trying right now."

"Why can't you imagine moving back home?"

"This is our home now and my career is here."

"My career is here as well, but I could easily move back down, and you could work with your father again..."

"You're fucking joking?" Nate turned to look out his passenger window.

"We're not going to do that. Please talk to me respectfully. Your father must be waiting to retire-you could have a beautiful career in Miami. You loved interior design."

"He's definitely not waiting to retire and you're the one who pushed me to become an artist."

"Same, same. Stop thinking about your potato pamphlets for a moment. I'm talking about us. I wanted you with me in New York, but it's not working out so let's get it together."

Nate sat up finding a seated position that was staunch in comparison to his earlier leaning re-cline, allowing the iPod to slip onto the floor with a thud.

"Please pay attention to the road," he said firmly.

"I want to have this out now."

"Why are you itching to fight on the way to our lovers' retreat? We are past this... this squabbling..."

"You might be past this— but I still have some processing to do. New York is different." Kate's right hand let go of the steering wheel and she reached for Nate's left hand.

"I lived in South Beach...gayer if anything. And I'm having some trouble with you mentioning it again. We discussed this thoroughly in therapy. You agreed and we said no more regression."

Kate turned to see his face.

"Just looking ahead now... Watch out!"

There was the brightness of headlights and a loud fearsome noise followed by various honking sounds, almost all of them different, resonating through the warm morning air. Two miles before their exit, their car swerved off the right side of the road, across the double yellow lines into the oncoming traffic, causing a collision and hurling Nate and Kate forward through a wormhole.

27

Second Chances

Nathan woke up alone again this morning, sullenly, sour-mouthed and eager to lift himself off the sweat-soaked sheets. The comforter layered with a blanket was too heavy and fought him when he tried to remove it from his body, he grabbed it firmly with a clenched fist and then pushed off its warm inertia before finally flinging the corner onto the other side of his lonely bed. It was still somewhat early for the weekend; Nathan decided early better than too late. His morning shower was cold and abrupt. The coffee on the other hand, was sweeter than usual, expressing the roasted bean flavor in his whole mouth, grounding him with contentment. Then some delightful toast and jam with enough sweetness to wake him. Just as he rose up off his seat at the kitchen table, his cellphone rang out with a plucky sound. Marimba. It took a moment to coordinate his movements until he followed the sound to the phone laying on the coffee table in the living room where he had left it the night before. There you are, his mind exclaimed and he lifted the phone and pressed the green circle on the touchscreen to answer.

"Are you up yet?" Katy was exceptionally cheerful that morning. Her voice was vibrant, the sun radiating above her as she drove across the Venetian Crossway.

"I've been up for at least a two hours."

"Liar."

"Whatever."

"You whatever. Did you have your cocktail?"

"They don't call it that anymore. Injection or just call it meds... in the butt. It's been working."

"I believe you."

"I feel wonderful and I just sold that portrait of you and thank Lakshmi. I was thinking of jumping out a window or something."

"Lakshmi again?"

"It's her."

"Jesus doesn't do it for you?"

"Not since the trip to India. I wore red special—she's always portrayed in red gowns. So many peacocks in Jaipur you wouldn't believe."

"What portrait of me? Why are you constantly painting me?"

"You're my lovely and I'm obsessed. That's why… it's a good one. The one where you're in your yellow swimsuit and the blue sky is so bright behind you."

"I look like I was repeatedly punched in the face in that one."

"You look beautiful and who cares-it sold."

"How's your new husband-Bobby-Benny…?"

"Brandon. Never around really. We had dinner last Tuesday before his redeye to the new L.A. gallery."

"No snuggles that night?"

"No snuggles that night, unfortunately, non of the dalliance. He keeps me hurting for affection."

"That Meanie."

"It's a good thing we never got married."

"That would have been wild."

"We fooled around that one night after our first date. I was really good you said." You could almost hear a note of pride from Nathan.

"I most definitely remember that night. The lava cake was so delicious. Why don't you come back down to Miami?"

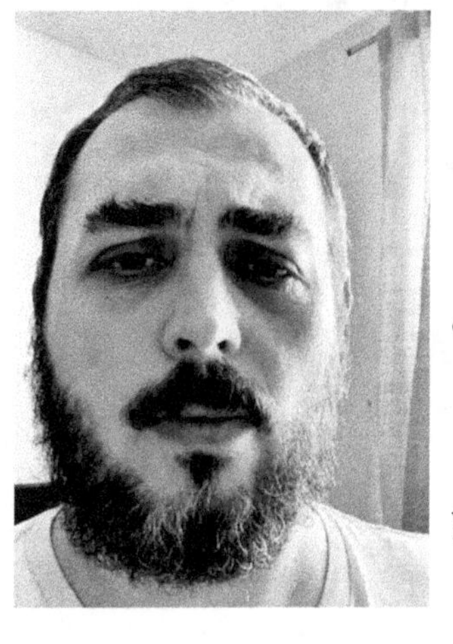

Slava Korin is an artist, designer and writer.

Other books authored by Slava Korin:
Sizzle
Twirling,   Shaking, Swaying
Down the Rabbit Hole
Gaslight